I0532855

HINNOM
MAGAZINE

December 2017
ISSUE 004

Edited by C.P. Dunphey

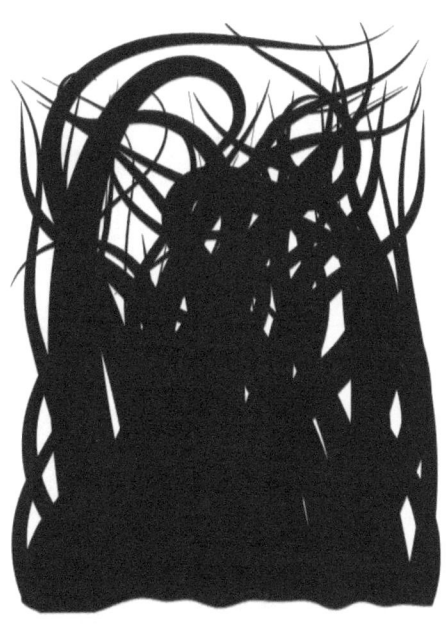

Gehenna & Hinnom Books

Table of Contents:

'Tis the Season of the Weird

Introduction by C.P. Dunphey

Welcome to Gehenna & Hinnom.

There is something unique about our culture's association with horror and the holidays. When the temperatures drop, and the snow starts to fall, horror is in the air. In recent memory, we've had films like *Krampus* (2015) to quench our morbid thirsts while we sip hot chocolate from our warm blankets. What is even more interesting is the history behind the titular character of that film. Its legend is one of terror, and its methods of punishing children during the holiday season are twisted. Saint Nicholas's foil, if you will. Pagan holiday celebrations, not just of Krampus, have been around a lot longer than we credit. So why the dark, twisted relation to what is supposed to be a season of joy? Is it because as humans we need to balance emotional highs with emotional lows? Is it because we are naturally pessimistic and need to see evil where there is so much good? Or, is it all completely irrelevant?

I believe that we attract ourselves to horror this time of the season because we are reaching the end of the year. All of the stress, all the events that have flown by, the work, the frustrations and anxiety, all boiling together until we can be born anew, just like the leaves that grow and flourish once more as the snow melts. Horror has always been a psychological weapon that mankind uses to express, and sometimes repress, subconscious and conscious feelings. We use horror as a conduit to express what we feel, especially when we are too afraid to utter it aloud. Reaching the end of the year is weight off the shoulders, but it is also a reminder of all that's come before it.

As we reach this end, I do reflect. On all the amazing people I have met as we raised Gehenna & Hinnom from the earth, together. Never in a million years did I think we would receive the response we did. Each and every author who had faith in us humbled me, to extents I don't believe I could explain even if I wanted to. A lot of work? Yes. Stressful? Definitely. Worth it? Absolutely. As G&H strolls into the new year, the stories of 100+ authors are what we reflect on. The beautiful, elaborate stories that they felt we would enjoy. The thousands of others who submitted as well, who had faith in our company.

You are all the reason we started this company, why we continue to grow this company, and why there is an ever-expanding base of readers who enjoy these strange, haunting tales.

'Tis the season of the weird. I am glad we could be weird together.

Enquiries from the Deep:

An Interview with Dark Fiction Titan John Langan

(Originally published in The Gehenna Post)

CP: You have had an incredibly successful past few years. Between *The Fisherman* winning the Bram Stoker Award for Best Novel and the releases of your short story collections, along with the reprinting of *House of Windows*. In both novels, you mention the long processes you've faced in completing these works. The meticulous nature of your language and structure shows careful planning and execution, unwavering patience, one could say. Could you delve a little into the creations of your novels? The struggles you've faced and the rewards that've come from your hard work?

JL: I suppose I should start by saying that I compose in longhand, on legal pads. When I wrote *House of Windows* and the first hundred pages or so of *The Fisherman*, I had a goal of one new page and one revised page per day. Each morning, I would wake up early—before, I liked to say, my internal editor was conscious—and rewrite the last page I'd written the previous day, cleaning it up and expanding it as I went, then moving onto a new page. If I felt at any point that the narrative had gone off track in some way, I would retrace my steps to the spot that had happened, and start over from there. Occasionally, I would jot down notes in the margins of the pages. For *House of Windows*, I wound up drawing a map of the layout of Belvedere House; for *The Fisherma*n, I sketched Apophis. By the time I came to complete *The Fisherman*, my daily method had changed slightly: now I concentrated on producing one new page each day, revising it as I went. Once each hand-written manuscript was complete, I typed it into the computer, submitting it to another round of revisions in the process. When the books were done, my wife read them and gave me feedback on them, which I used for another set of revisions before sending the books to my agent. *House of Windows* went through one more round of revisions, after a first round of submissions to major presses failed to yield any acceptances. The narrative that comprises the majority of the book originally was told in more or less chrono-logical order; I rearranged it to place the fight between Roger and Ted at the beginning.

I'm not sure my struggles writing the novels were any different from any other writer's. There was the same effort to see the narrative through to the end, to get right details of character and setting, to avoid easy shortcuts. As for rewards: there's the satisfaction of work well done, which should not be underestimated. When I was writing *House of Windows*, I said I wanted to write a book that, were I to be hit by a bus the day after I completed it, I could be happy to leave behind. I accomplished that. With *The Fisherman*, I borrowed advice the great Jeffrey Ford had given to my friend Laird Barron and wrote for broke, so to speak. I didn't hold anything back. With each book, I've had the experience of flipping to a random page and thinking, "Hey, this isn't bad." Which is nice.

CP: In both novels, your prose—as many have before stated—resembles the nature of more classical works. You've also openly spoken of the challenges you faced when finding the right publisher who understood the scope and unique voice that your fiction embodies. How did you come to find this voice in your writing? Has it always been there, or did it develop as you found your individuality as an author?

JL: I've always loved language, loved it when it's extravagant, florid, excessive. I grew up reading the Marvel comics of the 1960's and -70's, and I adored Stan Lee's hyperbolic, overheated style. The Mighty Thor and his quasi-Shakespearean pronouncements, the Silver Surfer and his sententious philosophizing, not to mention, the narrative Lee supplied for all the Marvel books, was as much a source of pleasure to me as the art of Jack Kirby and John Buscema. I loved the stately grandeur of Tolkien, who was one of the first prose writers I was aware of (thanks to the animated adaptations of *The Hobbit* and *The Lord of the Rings* when I was in grade school). During my teens, I gravitated to Stephen King's colloquial storytelling and Peter Straub's careful prose, as well as T.E.D. Klein's mannered style (with some Charlotte Bronte thrown in for good measure). College brought me to Faulkner and Henry James, grad school to Dickens and Woolf. All of which is to say that I drew a good deal of my inspiration and sustenance as a writer from reading writing that was distinguished by its attention to language. For me, style is an inextricable part of what I'm trying to do as a writer. I'm always happy whenever someone notices the care I've paid to it.

CP: I've found a consistent element in your works, throughout both your novels and short fiction, that I find very interesting. The details you evoke, the descriptions you so perfectly illustrate, craft imagery and scenery as if you were speaking of experience rather than a fictional story. Many say that method actors often *become* the characters in which they play, and I firmly believe that writers can become *method authors* with their stories, transporting themselves to these settings, into these experiences. Could you walk us through the process of your imagination when writing? Do the details appear on their own, flourish, and write themselves? Do they come from real-life experiences? If so, how and why, do you think?

JL: I'm tempted to quote Joseph Conrad here, his famous statement about his goal as a writer being to make you see what he sees as he sees it. There's a whole aesthetic there which gets worked out in his approach to fiction, and which you see in writers such as Dickens, James, and Faulkner. I suppose I think of the writer as the one who notices things, specifically, the things that will bring alive a particular scene for the reader. But that's an expression of their individual sensibility, isn't it?

All of this is a bit general, I realize; perhaps a bit of personal reflection would be useful. I see my process as a writer as having developed a bit over the last decade and a half. When I started, I tended to think very deliberately about the story I was going to write, using the particular monster at its heart as a way of focusing my attention. A monster such as the mummy, say, tends to bring with it certain plot movements, certain imagery, and I used those conventions as a kind of frame to build my narrative on, even when I was working against or at cross-purposes to them. I didn't write outlines for my stories, but I frequently discussed them with my wife when we were in the car, kicking around ideas with her. As we did so, the characters revealed themselves to me, beginning a process that continued as I sat down to write the story. I was aware that many of those characters shared certain personality traits, interests, or experiences with me, or that they had been inspired in some way by people I knew, but I also wanted my characters to have their own, distinct existences. As much as anything, I found each story needed a particular narrative voice, which tended to come to me in the first line and proceed from there. I don't know that I thought about it in these terms at the time, but my goal was very much to inhabit the story, all the way down to the level of language.

In more recent years, I've become interested in writing stories that draw more directly on my autobiography, perhaps because I feel more confident in my ability to treat that material. I've become aware that everything is a potential source for a story, from half-remembered fragments from my childhood to overheard snippets of conversation. I've said before that, the more I write, the more I find I can write, and that seems more true to me now than ever.

CP: I've seen where many have said, in agreement with our own statements in our reviews, that your work stands on its own, despite the weird and literary inspirations. Your novels and short fiction are original, frightening, and unforgettable. In the age of the New Weird, and with the flood of Lovecraftian inspiration in recent memory, how can authors attain individuality while maintaining affection for their inspirations? What are some techniques that help you capture that signature voice and the enthralling concepts we've come to love so much, while presenting the stories in a fresh, innovative manner?

JL: I think all art begins in imitation of other art. How else are you supposed to learn how to write a story but by reading other stories and doing what they do? I'm all for Jonathan Lethem's idea of the ecstasy of influence, of embracing your influences with full enthusiasm, and writing through them to find your own style. As I see it, art is made of art; there's no such thing as a pure, uncontaminated style. What is distinctive is the way in which your particular sensibility assembles its influences into a whole. Don't fret so much about originality; instead, dive into what you love and absorb yourself in it, let it absorb you. Remain open to new things, allow them to interact with what's inside you already. Embrace your passions.

CP: Bouncing off of your response of "inhabit(ing) the story," I feel the need to mention the world-building in *The Fisherman*. You have a knack for unorthodox narrative structures, with a large part of *The*

Fisherman delving into the story that Abe and Dan hear in the diner concerning the Reservoir, and then with *House of Windows* and its story-within-a-story structure. Whereas *House of Windows* uses a lot of real locations, *The Fisherman* takes some creative liberties. How did you find yourself building the history of Dutchman's Creek? What led to the decision to make the retelling of the story such a large section of the book?

JL: I'm fascinated by stories. I grew up with parents who were both storytellers, and I've always loved narratives in which characters tell stories to one another (i.e. *Heart of Darkness, Ethan Frome, My Antonia, The Great Gatsby, Ghost Story, Pet Sematary*, etc.). I still love it when a friend or family member tells a story. My first two published horror stories, "On Skua Island" and "Mr. Gaunt," make use of the story-within-a-story structure, so it came readily to hand when I began what would become my novels. In the cases of both *House of Windows* and *The Fisherman*, though, I thought the internal stories would be significantly shorter than they turned out to be. I should clarify here that, when I started each book, I expected it would be some variety of shorter narrative, most likely a novelette, maybe a novella. I had no plans for either to grow to novel length. This happened because each internal story kept revealing more of itself to me, expanding and deepening. In turn, this pushed the narratives in the direction of the novel. It also required an increasing amount of research. In the case of *The Fisherman*, I consulted a few local histories and watched a documentary on the construction of the Ashokan Reservoir. The idea was always for the past story to add resonance and significance to the events of the present story; otherwise, you would have a strange and not entirely satisfactory narrative. As much as I could, I kept the events of *The Fisherman*'s internal narrative within the larger bounds of the actual building of the reservoir. What I wound up with was a book that was really a novella within a novella, but I decided I was happy with that structure.

CP: As an experienced writer of both novels and shorter fiction, which one do you enjoy more? Do you have a specific story or work that you favor more than others? Why or why not?

JL: All of my stuff tends to be long; even when I'm writing a story for an anthology, it's likely to fall within novelette territory (and increasingly novella). Writing a true short story that succeeds as such is something I've managed maybe a handful of times, possibly a little more. I tend to prefer to work at length; I enjoy the feeling of being able to explore character and situation in depth. My favorite story tends to change depending on the day, but I'm very fond of one called "Homemade Monsters" that appeared in Ellen Datlow's *The Doll Collection* a couple of years ago, in part because it features Godzilla.

CP: With the difficulties you've faced in finding the right publisher for your works, and the success you eventually met when things aligned, did you develop any belief of the importance of being honest as a writer? Many might've felt they needed to alter their story or language to meet the expectations of the publishers and a lot of new authors may struggle with having their voices disliked or criticized. What are your thoughts on remaining true to yourself as an author, and concerning the importance of perseverance?

JL: I was fortunate in having found receptive editors for my stories pretty much from the start, in the form of Gordon Van Gelder, John Joseph Adams, and Ellen Datlow. Their support of what I was doing, no matter how bizarre, was a big help when I was trying to find homes for both my novels. I was also lucky to have friends such as Laird Barron and Paul Tremblay.

When it comes right down to it, though, you have to believe in what you're doing. You have to expect that what you write isn't going to be to everyone's taste, and you have to be able to accept that and move on from it. There's no point in chasing publishing trends; it's better to try to write the best story or novel that you can write. A few years ago, Laird Barron pointed out something to me: if you go to Goodreads or Amazon and look at the ratings for a book such as Peter Straub's *Ghost Story*, you'll see that they fall at about the three-star range. If you check the reviews themselves, you'll find a fair number of four- and five-star reviews, but you'll also find an astonishing number of one- and two-star ratings, with the comments to go with them. If a modern classic such as *Ghost Story* can receive this kind of treatment, then you have to be prepared for what you write to attract the same knocks.

I guess this is one advantage of having studied English lit: I'm familiar with the idea that a writer's success is not a foregone conclusion. Think of Melville: we consider him one of our greatest novelists, but his reputation didn't begin its ascent until he'd been dead for about thirty years. This isn't to sound overly pessimistic, but it is to say, if you're writing for immediate widespread praise, you may want to reconsider that.

CP: *The Fisherman* was released just last year, the new printing of *House of Windows* back in July of this year. Despite the recent timings of these releases, do you have anything cooking in the pot? What can readers look forward to in 2018 from John Langan?

JL: I'm just about done with the new stories that will go into my third collection of stories, *Sefira and Other Betrayals*, which should then be out from Hippocampus Press in the late winter/early spring. I'll also have stories in a couple of Ellen Datlow's anthologies later in the year.

CP: We always like to end our interviews with a question for the readers. As many of our readers are authors themselves, I wanted to ask you: If there was one bit of advice you could give to a fledgling writer, what would it be?

JL: Write what you love. Be brave. Spend less time on social media, more time reading.

DAD'S FAMOUS PRESERVES
By Seras Nikita

When I was eleven, and my brother Rourke was sixteen, Dad moved us to the jungle to deliver the Lord's Good Word to the people who lived there.

He must have thought it would change us. Make us into men, lift us above the everyday sins of the other boys littering the stoops of Boston.

That's what he called them—*everyday sins.*

Dad said that everyday sins were small things.

Small things, like not telling the Irish girl who lives in the building across the way that the cat's been sitting in her window, because the way her curtains fall lately they bunch up around the pull-string, and if a person were bending down in just the right way, for example on his knees whispering prayers before bed, he might see right through the gap to whomever might be standing there blow-drying her hair in clean white panties.

"Everyday sins can sneak up on you, son. Like bees. One or two aren't so bad, but when you get a swarm of them together you're in big trouble."

Dad had black hair and a mouth that could smile all the way to the corners of his eyes. He was not a religious fanatic or a child abuser, if that's what you're thinking. Dad never beat us with Bibles or locked us in closets or forced us to grasp crucifixes heated over burners. He was just an electrician turned preacher who, in addition to being fond of analogies, believed that God would want men and boys to wear heeled shoes and pressed shirts while they were delivering the Good News.

He'd been flipping a batch of Dad's Famous Hotcakes while he delivered the analogy about the bees. Dad cooked us hot meals all the time, and everything he made was "Famous."

"They'll sting you swollen, son, if you give them a chance. You have to be on the lookout."

He put the plate of hotcakes on the table and we ate them together in the warm kitchen with syrup and butter and cold milk.

There were no bees in the jungle.

The native women were not like the Irish girl or the lady with the tiny waist on the detergent box. Their breasts fell to their navels like cupfuls of cold molasses sinking slowly down their chests. They were the first breasts I'd ever seen up close. Instead of using a toilet the villagers squatted over holes, and their nails were thick and yellow. They were all missing a toenail or a fingernail, and sometimes more than one. The girls poked pieces of wood and bone through holes in their noses and ears, and sometimes lumps of scar tissue bloomed up around the holes like the chunks of white lime built up around our drain at home. They squatted next to coal beds while they cooked. Some nights the firelight showed me their down-there hair and dark parts that hung beneath like flaps. Some had brown and black tattoos on their faces. Some of their heads were as bald as eggs.

The men were strong and glossy and hard. They hunted monkeys and butchered them with their hands. Then they cooked up the meat, and the guts too. They even broke open the bones and dug inside with their thumbs, and then ate the stuff that came out. Sometimes they pulled out the guts before the monkey even stopped breathing.

The children turned over logs and found white grubs the size of pecans that they roasted on sticks before chewing them up. They watched the moon and some nights they smeared things on themselves and danced in front of bonfires. One night, I saw a baby born.

Inside our chapel was very, very hot. The walls and roof were made of heavy pine planks.

"The planks were the first thing we brought in once the road was cleared," said Father Claussen, showing us how to fan out mosquito nets over our beds and weight them at the bottom. He pointed to the four glass windows, looking very proud.

"From a pair of very charitable Christians in Long Island. Real glass. They let the light of Christ shine right in." He beamed. "I doubt there's another set of glass windows for three hundred miles in any direction."

The windows didn't open. The air in the chapel was as hot and heavy as the steam that used to hiss from Dad's iron. Beads of sap oozed from the pine lumber, scenting the smother like Christmastime. Everything was sticky. The few villagers curious enough to attend the services brought banana leaves to sit on, so they wouldn't get sap on their bottoms from sitting in the pews. They fanned themselves with fronds and then stopped coming altogether.

Dad said sometimes the Good Word was like the sound of the ocean.

"Waves just keep crashing on in the background, and finally a day comes when people see that the waters are cool and clear. People wade in and try to swim. Some of those people will take to the water like fish, and others might not get the hang of it right away. Some people might only dip in a toe." He'd always drop his voice for the next part. "And some people need us more than anyone else, because by the time they get to the water they've already been on fire for a long, long time."

Dad was from Chicago first, then Minneapolis, and then Boston. He'd signed a year contract for us, and when the review board asked if he had any experience living in the tropical wild, he said, "I've studied up." Then to us, he said, "If the Swiss Family Robinson can do it, so can we. The Lord will watch over us." But not many days had passed before it became clear that neither was true. We were dangerously ignorant about the jungle.

We'd packed useless things. A swimsuit. A gold pocket watch. A red plastic radio that never picked up a station and ran out of batteries after the first week. Dad brought three jars of Brylcream, because he was afraid he'd run out. Nonetheless, he assured us, everything would be okay. We were on the Lord's mission and He was looking out for us.

Those first few months were a dark time. Our water filter was a heavy contraption that took both hands and all my weight to pump. In the heat of the day, I'd avoid pumping water until I was so thirsty my head throbbed, and then make it worse by exerting myself in the heat. For food, we had a kind of dried porridge with vitamins ground up in it, and you added water to make a sweet, gritty sludge. The best way to get it down was to drink it fast, like codliver oil.

Suffering in button-up shirts and heeled shoes with socks, we doled out litanies to the strange natives who looked at us skeptically, clucking their tongues and shaking their heads. The village children ran naked in the open air, and waded into the brown running stream to splash their dark bodies with water. I tried not to feel bitter thoughts toward them.

On Sundays Dad offered Sacrament, pressing wafers of host into rough, brown hands and making the sign of the cross in the air. "On the night in which he was betrayed, Christ broke bread and said, Take and Eat. This is my Body, given for you. Do this in remembrance of Me." The villagers inspected the paper discs, taking wary nibbles as if tasting an unfamiliar fruit for the first time without knowing if the flesh would send them into fits or cause chaos in their bowels. Nobody understood a word either side was saying.

At night Roarke and I lay beneath the mosquito nets and felt things crawling on us, scratching furrows in our legs with our grimy fingernails. We'd been itchy and paranoid since the night Roarke had found a millipede as long as his forearm coiled inside his pillowcase. Sometimes we lay in bed and remembered things together, like the icebox back in Boston and the cool fountain in the square. Rory reminded me of Dad's Famous Potato-and-Fried-Egg-Hash with Catsup, and I reminded him of Dad's Famous Chocolate Egg Cream, always with an extra sprinkle of Ovaltine on top.

One very dark night I dreamed of the Irish girl. She was blow-drying her hair. She turned around, and I saw that her breasts were deformed and made of scar tissue, lumps stacked upon lumps like bunches of half-dried grapes. Beneath her white panties something bulged and squirmed. The hard, horny head of a giant millipede emerged from one leg of her panties and wound down the inside of her thigh, circling once before disappearing behind her knee. She held up her thumb, and there was black stuff on it. She sucked it off and smiled, looking right at me, still holding the blow dryer.

I'd wet the bed that night for the first time in years, but Rory didn't notice. The sheets were always damp anyway, and we'd trained our noses not to smell things.

Four months passed, and Dad was sick. He would stand in the palmettos behind the chapel and make himself vomit before morning service, so he wouldn't have to stop the sermon when he felt it coming. Long, flat worms like ribbons came up in the vomit. Yellow stains bloomed in the armpits of his white shirts, and he had to go to the bathroom all the time. He grew thin and grim.

Still, he didn't want to leave. He said that nothing was more transient than flesh, and he felt proud that God believed he was strong enough to be tested.

Rory and I wondered about this. We also wondered whether or not God considered all meat to be flesh. Were the worms made of flesh? Were the grubs, the millipede? The monkey guts? Were the villagers? What was the difference between flesh, and just regular old meat? We couldn't decide.

The infection began with a black dot the size of a pea on the top of Dad's foot. It looked like the time I'd stepped on a sharpened pencil, and a smooth pellet of lead had lodged itself in the web of my big toe.

At first, it only itched. Dad thought it might be a mosquito bite turned blood-blister. Maybe he could just coax out a few drops of blood, and the thing would turn back into regular skin. He squeezed it between his thumbnails, but nothing came out.

When it was bigger the next day, he tried to prick it with the corner of his folding razor. The blade barely brushed the dot before Dad sucked air over his teeth and squeezed his eyes shut, gripping the sides of his foot with both hands as if curling up that way would make the pain stop.

The next day the dot was twice as big, and it was no longer a dot. It was a little brown crater with a black pit, and the ring of skin around the crater was puffy and angry-looking. The day after that the foot was so swollen it bulged out of Dad's shoe like rising bread, and a day after *that* the shoe didn't fit at all.

For the first time in four months, Dad stayed in his bed beneath the mosquito net instead of rising for morning prayer. We tried to cool him by fanning him with fronds, the way the villagers did. We pumped the water filter for him and offered him mangos and porridge. He drank some water and ate a little of the mango, but the porridge came right back up.

When he could no longer bear the heat in the chapel, he crawled outside to lie on the ground in the shade of the giant palmettos. His hair hung in greasy strings and his forehead was shiny with oil and sweat. The whites of his eyes had begun to look yellowish. He was embarrassed that he'd had to crawl.

Two days later, Dad didn't even think about crawling. All day long he lay moaning under the palmettos with a mosquito net draped over him, not caring about the ants that marched across his belly or the centipedes making paths through his hair. He kept one hand pressed into his face, either palm-down covering his eyes or palm-out with the back of it pressing into his mouth. I think he did that so no more pain sounds would come out.

Dad hadn't taken off his sock. He couldn't; the rapid swelling had cinched the seam of elastic tightly around his calf. Flesh bulged above and below the seam, making Dad's lower leg look like a tied sausage.

We could have cut the sock off. Despite our ill preparedness in other areas, we'd managed to bring a pocketknife apiece. Roarke's even had a tiny pair of scissors that folded out, so you could pinch them open and closed with your thumb and forefinger. But Dad wouldn't let us touch his sock. I think he was afraid to see what was happening under there. He didn't want Rory and me to see, either, but we knew it was worse than we could imagine because by then the smell was so bad.

Dad's infected leg gave off a stench like fetid cheese and rotten hamburger meat. You could smell it ten feet away. We'd all done a fine job of training our noses to ignore our own smelly underarms and the bouquet of the latrine-hole, but no sane person could ever shut out the smell of Dad's infected leg. My brother and I stole sips of air through our mouths and pretended we didn't notice as we sat with Dad, distracting him with staged arguments about which of his sermons we remembered best. He distracted us with forced chuckles that doubled him fetal with pain.

Dad's moans became high and shrill at the end. Consumed, none of us ate or slept. Rory and I didn't know what was expected of us, and Dad was too sick to say. God was nowhere to be found.

After Dad slipped into delirium, he could no longer refuse Roarke's pleas to let him run and fetch Father Claussen. Rory left the chapel early in the morning, disappearing into the spots of brush that had grown over the path since we'd walked it last. He didn't come back until dawn.

"Father Claussen will be here when the sun comes up. He'll bring some men with a cart and a mule to bring Dad out. "

I lifted the mosquito net, so Rory could climb into bed next to me.

"What about a doctor?" I whispered.

"There isn't one." Rory groaned softly as he settled into the bed. He sounded very tired. "Not a real one. Dad'll have to be flown out the way we came in. Father Claussen's already radioed San Tomás for a pilot." Rory was silent for a while. "I told Father Claussen about . . . about the smell. He asked me how long, and I told him almost a week." After another pause Rory added quietly, "He asked me if we have kin in Boston. You know . . . just in case . . . in case Dad. . ." Rory broke off in a heave. I could tell he wanted to cry. At last he said, "In case the Lord takes Dad before we make it out of here." He said that in an even, weighted voice I'd never heard from Roarke before. Dad was right about one thing. The jungle had made a man of my brother.

A Presbyterian doctor in San Tomás cut off Dad's pants with scissors that were bent flat halfway down so they could slide right between Dad's pants and his leg. Then the doctor used his bent scissors to cut Dad's sock into squares. When he began to peel away the squares, Dad tore at his sheets and screamed to God for the strength to stand it until a nurse rushed in with more morphine.

Father Claussen stood by his head and Rory and I held Dad's hands as each square was peeled away. His leg didn't look like a leg anymore. The knee was a black bulge with hard, raised bruises. In the gaps between bruises were mounds of flesh so swollen that the skin over them was stretched white and split into hard bloodless cracks. Below the knee the bruises became a forest of brown craters, each with a black pit, like the first one we'd seen on the top of Dad's foot. The one he thought might be a mosquito bite.

Square by square, the infection only grew more grotesque. Ripe pustules on the calf broke audibly to drip green fluid that filled the room with its cheesy, sickening smell. Around the ankles, thick white and yellow stuff pooled between chunks of diseased tissue. The foot was nothing more than a spongy grayish mass, like a wet biscuit dissolving in mop water.

A lot of the squares wouldn't peel off. They were melded to the leg with crumbles of yellow crust, and trying to peel them just caused more flesh to tear away, exposing Dad's long white leg bone. The doctor called the squares of stuck sock 'grafted,' and said that it probably happened at the very beginning, before Dad's body stopped trying to scab over and heal itself. The doctor gave up trying to remove the remaining squares of sock. Even he looked aghast.

"I've never seen anything like it," he kept saying. His accent sounded like the man with the hotdog cart back home. "I've never seen anything like it."

Father Claussen took us into a waiting room and swallowed an aspirin and told us that the 'grafted' squares of sock didn't matter anyway.

"I'm not a doctor," he said, "But if I've ever seen a clear-cut case for amputation it was lying in front of me ten minutes ago." Father Claussen sank into a chair and looked at my brother and I, thin and filthy, blotchy with heat rash and covered with the scabs of bug bites scratched bloody in the night. I could tell by the way he softened that he pitied us. "San Tomás has some of the best doctors in this part of the world," he said. "If your father's life is meant to be saved, these men will save it." The priest closed his eyes and I knew he was seeing it again, Dad's rotting leg. I saw it too. It was burned into the dark behind our eyelids. He tightened his hold on the crucifix around his neck. Then he opened his eyes and looked at us sincerely. His voice was as soft as a whisper.

"Your father should not be alive. God is truly walking with this man."

God may have been walking with Dad that day, but Dad himself would never walk again. The doctors found rot running all the way up to his hip, so that's where they amputated. The place where Dad's leg once met his pelvis was now just a concave socket the size of a baby's head, with prickly stitches like long black caterpillars holding the skin in place. There was a tube in Dad's arm for morphine and fluids, one in his chest to pump antibiotics in, and another beneath the covers to pump other things out.

A long time passed before Dad was conscious enough to speak. Father Claussen made arrangements for us to stay at a convent in San Tomás, where the nuns treated us like children. They did not know the things we had seen.

When Dad started to come around, the doctor called Father Claussen and he drove us from the convent to the hospital in his big green Buick. I stood beside Dad's bed so excited I began to cry. Dad opened his eyes, then closed them for so long I was afraid he'd drifted off again. But at last he broke the seal of scum cementing his lips together and the first thing he said was:

"Where is it?"

Father Claussen looked at us and we both shrugged our shoulders.

"Dad," Rory said gently with tears on his cheeks, "We're here. Simon and I and Father Claussen. You're going to be all right." Rory's throat caught, and he glanced at the lopsided mound of blankets covering Dad's lower body. "I mean, you're going to make it. You're not going to die."

Dad didn't say anything for a minute. I squeezed his hand. His head turned on his pillow and he looked at me incredulously.

"Didn't you hear me ask you a question, son? I said—where the fuck is my goddamned leg?"

Back in the waiting room, the doctor with the accent and the bent scissors spoke to Father Claussen in a rapid, rolling language. Father Claussen looked at the floor with his hands clasped behind his back, nodding. When the doctor was finished, the priest turned to us and said, "The doctors think that your father's fever has damaged part of his brain."

I stammered, stunned and confused. But Roarke was angry. His fists were tight balls at his sides.

"The problem with our Dad was his leg, Father. Or didn't you see it? Because I did. And my little brother sure did. A fever can't change a person that way. When I had the mumps, I was as hot as a skillet for three days, couldn't bear a stitch of clothing or a spoonful of broth, and I didn't wake up a swearing blasphemer."

Father Claussen nodded, still looking at the floor, this time with his hands clasped in front of him. He started to say something, then stopped, as if he'd changed his mind about what to say. He started again, carefully.

"Son, every part of a man is controlled by a specific part of his brain. When one part of the brain is damaged, he might forget how to walk. Another part, and he forgets how to swallow, or how to speak, or how to read or write or do arithmetic.

"These doctors say that sometimes—not very often, but sometimes—a very special part of the brain gets hurt, and the person forgets what kind of person he is. They think that in your dad's case, the fever just... burned that part of him away." Father Claussen put his hand on Rory's shoulder. "May God be with you boys. The Church will do everything it can to help you and your father through this trial. You must have faith."

Roarke clenched his fists more tightly and shrugged out from under Father Claussen's hand.

"God had his chance, Father. And the Church brought us to this Gomorrah to begin with. I don't think we'd like any help from either of you. In fact, I think my brother and I ought to be alone right now." He took me by the arm and began to turn away.

Father Claussen's voice called out,

"This is a time for joining together in prayer, not for casting blame."

Roarke did not turn back.

"There is one more thing," called the priest. Something in his voice made Rory stop.

"Your father says he won't leave here without his leg."

The man in the hospital bed had Dad's face, but nothing else about him was the same. When the nurses came to change his bandages, he waited until they were leaning over him before he tweaked their nipples through their smocks and asked if all the women from their country were sluts-on-wheels-with-titties-of-steel. He held his fork with the wrong hand and laughed at things that weren't funny. He wanted to know where the fuck were his goddamn cigarettes, wide-filter Pall Malls, as if he'd smoked them every day of his life.

Even his breath smelled different. I know because right before we landed in Massachusetts, he grabbed my collar and pulled me close.

"Those olive-eatin' sawbones said they'd never seen the fuckin' bug I got," he told me, his voice low. He was so close I could feel hot breath in my nostrils. "Said maybe it was the first time anyone got it, anywhere in the whole world. And I said isn't that something? Hey, why don't you pack the whole thing up and ship it back to the good old U.S. of A? Maybe have the fellas from the Mayo take a look at it? For research, you know? Just so I can make sure I do my part." He smiled a smile that made his face dark. "Then I look at the sawbones with my eyes real big . . . big wide crocodile eyes . . . and I say, I wanna do my part to see this tragedy don't befall another living soul. Not if I can do anything about it." He laughed sweetish breath into my face and I recoiled. He yanked me fiercely back to him. "It belongs to me, after all. It's my goddamned *leg.* You can't just toss someone's leg in the garbage like a used rubber. So they said yeah, maybe I had a point. Those brains at the Mayo are thinking up new medicine all the time. Pills to stop your headache, cure the clap. Even pills to make your dick hard! Those guys may have something goin'. So the sawbones trussed it up in a big glass tube fulla some of that formaldehyde stuff. Locked it in with these big steel caps. I saw 'em loading it into the cargo hold. Looks like the biggest pickled pig's foot you ever saw." He laughed again. There was a rattle and a lurch as the landing gear deployed. We were back in Boston, but it didn't feel like home. Nothing was the same. "I'll be fucked if those needledicks at the Mayo will ever get their hands on it. It's mine." Dad pulled me so close his nose touched the skin of my forehead, and his voice fell to a whisper that made my skin break into gooseflesh. "Do you hear me, son? *It's mine.*"

Father Claussen had arranged a one-bedroom apartment for us on a sloppy street beside an Italian restaurant. It was close to Saint Elizabeth's, the hospital where Dad could go if he needed to see a doctor.

"And I mean the other sort of doctor too," Father Claussen reminded us. "A psychiatrist. If he gets any worse, or if you boys are ever afraid he'll hurt you, just pick up the phone and call Saint Elizabeth's right away. I've written the number to the psychiatric crisis line right here next to the phone." He also said the church would pay all of Dad's medical bills, so not to worry about that. And there was a Murphy bed in the living room, he told us, so there would be room for all of us as long as my brother and I shared a bed. He spoke a last hurried blessing, and then he left.

The apartment smelled like garlic bread and had nubby carpeting with gold and burgundy curlicues, like carpet from a movie theater lobby. There was something called a 'kitchenette,' which was a half-sized icebox, a sink and a hotplate on an island of dingy linoleum that curled up where it met the carpet.

Father Claussen said he chose this apartment because it had belonged to a man with polio. The door that led in from the alley had a wide ramp and a rail for Dad's wheelchair, and above the bathtub and toilet were special bars where he could grab on if he needed to. The countertops in the kitchen and bathroom were only half as high as normal so he could reach everything.

Dad sat in his wheelchair in the kitchenette smoking Pall Malls and yelling slurs at the two black porters who had toted our luggage from the airport. We didn't have much, mostly just secondhand clothes and dishes from the nuns in San Tomás. The pair of big men struggled up the wheelchair ramp with something heavy wrapped in black duvetyn. They set it down in the corner and were wiping their brows when Dad yelled,

"You stupid spooks! Are you gonna put that right in front of the radiator?" He dropped his cigarette in the sink and wheeled angrily across the room. "Be careful with that, goddamnit. Do you even know what this is?" He yanked off the duvetyn. Rory and I froze, staring, not believing. "It's my goddamned leg, that's what it is!"

There it was, Dad's rotten leg, bobbing inside a glass tube as high as my shoulders. Steel caps closed the tube at the top and bottom, bolted tight with pieces that looked like chrome lug nuts. A paper with a big orange symbol that said BIOHAZARD stuck to the glass with strips of wrinkly white tape, and a few paragraphs of medical words filled the space beneath the symbol. Beyond that, the gray mess of craters and boils floated like a fleshy jellyfish in the pale, yellow preservative.

"Cost me half my nutsack and a gold pocket watch. Good thing you darkies are hot for bribes and shiny things or it'd be halfway to Alabama by now, on its way to be poked apart by some egghead with a microscope up his ass." One of the black men took a step toward Dad, like he might hit him, but the other man touched his elbow and shook his head, and after that they both left, closed the door behind them.

The lights in our new apartment were dimmed by puddles of dead moths settled in their yellowed fixtures. The fluorescent over the kitchenette flickered constantly, like it was sucking its electricity through a bent straw. There was not enough light or space or air. We all stood together in our new home, not speaking. Me, my brother, my Dad and his preserved amputated leg.

Rory turned seventeen that spring and fibbed himself a year older so he could join the Navy. I cried and begged him not to leave, but he went anyway. He hugged me and told me he'd be back before I knew it, but he couldn't look me in the eye and we both knew he was abandoning me. He was leaving me alone with Dad.

Dad smoked cigarettes all day and watched game shows on TV. *The Price is Right* was his favorite, he said, because when Bob Barker picked a pretty woman to guess the prices you could see her tits bouncing as she ran down to the stage.

"Hell, doesn't even have to be a pretty one," he said, lighting a fresh cigarette off the old one.

We mostly ate take-out from White Castle and Carl's Jr., but sometimes at the end of the month before Dad's disability check arrived I'd use the hotplate to warm up food for us. Mostly frozen things: corndogs, pizzas, Marie Calendar's chicken pot-pies in flimsy tins made of foil. We'd eat off paper plates sitting at a card table we'd found folded up under Dad's bed. Once I'd tried to make beef stroganoff, but when the time came to eat it I couldn't. I couldn't get past the thick gravy and the slippery noodles sliding over bits of meat. After the stroganoff I had a hard time eating altogether. The feeling of chewed food churning around in my mouth made me sick to my stomach.

I lost weight. I took long baths and showers, liking the feeling of scrubbed skin and the closed door between me and Dad. In the afternoons I sat outside on the wheelchair ramp and pretended to read catalogues. From there I could see people walking past on the sidewalk, but they couldn't see me. I saw the public-school kids walking home from the bus stop, and housewives on their way back from the baker and the butcher. Once I thought I saw the Irish girl walking past with a loaf of French bread and a sack of tangerines, but I couldn't be sure it was her. I couldn't remember if I'd ever seen her face.

I slept long nights on the pilled mattress of the Murphy bed. Dad's leg glowered from its pedestal, a wooden occasional table with one wobbly leg that Dad had made Rory and me drag in off the curb. He said the table would hold fine as long as we propped the broken leg with a stack of flattened cigarette cartons, and it did.

My dreams were bad, and got worse as the summer wore on. The worst dream of all came on the night it happened, the night after the fourth of July. I remember because it was right before the heat wave broke. You remember—the bad one that tripped the grid and blacked out the entire east side.

Has it been over a month already? Christ. You lose track.

That night was the hottest night I'd seen since the chapel in the jungle. The apartment was stale and suffocating, and the reek of garlic and cigarettes and formaldehyde was everywhere. I felt miserable and feverish even after I'd stripped to my underwear and cranked the knob on the window fan as far as it would go. My stomach gnawed as I lay sleepless, watching red digits on the clock radio in the kitchenette stack minutes into hours. It was a little past three when I heard a crack like a gunshot—a transformer shorting out. The fan blades stopped whirring and all the streetlamps went dark. I'd never thought about how much light comes in through a person's windows, even with the curtains closed, but suddenly the whole apartment was black as pitch. The clock radio clicked into battery mode and its red glow gave shape to the card table, the icebox, the world's biggest pickled pig's foot. I heard the door to Dad's room creak open, telling me the transformer had woken him too, and he would need a couple cigarettes and a spoonful of Carnation and maybe half an hour on the toilet listening to his own satisfied grunts to soothe him back to sleep.

A sound came from the hall like something catching or dragging on the carpet. I tried to climb out of bed to help, thinking he'd wedged his wheels against the baseboards again. But as always happens in nightmares, I found myself fixed flat on my back, paralyzed and numb. The dragging sound grew louder and closer. I panicked. Fear swarmed through me and I screamed at my frozen muscles, *GET UP, JESUS, GET UP!* But my arms and legs were too heavy or too weak or too tired. My eyes raced to the only scrap of light, the red glow of the clock, and something was wrong. The light was all wrong. It wasn't doing something it usually did, wasn't casting the right shadow on the linoleum. It wasn't casting the shadow of . . . of the leg.

The leg was gone.

The steel caps were still locked tightly in place, but nothing floated in the yellow preservative except a layer of fallen-off bits that formed chunky sediment at the bottom of the tube. The dragging came again, this time right next to the Murphy bed. I squeezed my eyes shut, pressing hot tears between my eyelashes, and for the first time in a long time my lips moved silently in frantic prayer. Slowly, I rolled my eyes to the side of my head and I saw it, the ghastly rotten leg. It was coming for me, sliding through the dark, using the rubbery remains of its toes to drag itself across the rough theater lobby carpet. Strings of flesh and the knob of jellied femur left a trail of preservative to show where it had been.

And I could smell it. Not the formaldehyde smell but the smell from beneath the palmettos, the smell of maggots feasting on raw cheeseburgers, of flesh rotting in the tropical sun. I felt a tug at the sheets and the exposed knuckle of the leg's big toe appeared above the mattress. I felt myself losing it, delirious with fear. Then came the second toe, struggling over the hump, gripping the sheet like a monkey to pull itself up onto the mattress. The other toes followed as the leg slithered into bed with me. I gagged on the stench and the fear and the feel of spongy flesh against my belly. I couldn't move. I couldn't breathe. I was going to drown in fear. I shut my eyes and felt my heart thump out one more massive helping of blood, before everything went bright white.

And then I was awake. I leapt out of bed and wheeled around, sweeping my eyes to the tube in the corner. It bobbed there innocently in the red glow, as if to say, "See? I've been right here the whole time." The blood rushed from my head and I dropped to my hands and knees, weak. My ribs stood out from my chest as I breathed in and out. My heart skipped and started. I think I might have grayed out for a while.

I was so tired. So tired and so hungry and so weak. I looked up at the leg, hating it. I wanted everything back the way it was. I wanted to walk into our old kitchen and find Dad standing on two feet in front of the stove, flipping a batch of his Famous Hotcakes and practicing aloud his sermon for the day. I wanted Rory to come back and make me believe I wasn't alone anymore. I wanted to sink my teeth into a hamburger or a banana or a slice of roast beef without feeling my tongue begin to explore its imaginary craters and boils. I just wanted to be rid of it. *All of it.*

The tube was easier to break than you'd think. It really only took one good whack with the hotplate to shatter the entire thing.

Dad heard the noise, of course, but he must've considered his own obvious limitations, because he didn't even try to pull me off. He screamed curses at me from his wheelchair, and when that didn't work he dialed the number Farther Claussen had written next to the phone. Then you guys came, and brought me here. At first you strapped me to the bed, but I got that privilege back for good behavior. I'm not sure how long it took you guys to arrive after Dad called. I don't really remember that part at all. I expect it probably took longer than usual, on account of the blackout. All I remember is a terrible, throbbing urgency to have Dad back—the real Dad. The Dad who'd made us pancakes and hated the smell of ashtrays, and who stood sweating before a tribe of villagers, intent only on the word of God. The Dad who'd said in a voice I can now recall only as an echo: "Take, and Eat. This is my Body, given for you. Do this in remembrance of me."

Seras Nikita is a writer of horror and science fiction. She's published stories in magazines, anthologies, and podcasts including *Pseudopod, Nightmare Magazine, Body Parts Magazine,* and recently, *A Breath from the Sky* print horror anthology by Martian Migraine Press.

FISCHER'S MOUTH
By Timothy G. Huguenin

Every year, when the snow began to melt off the sunny side of the valley and trickle into the Augustus River, Fischer would grow a mouth on the inside of his forearm. It would disappear in about a week, as suddenly as it came. He didn't know why it came or why it went; it was just a quirk of his identity that he had come to accept.

It was an obnoxious-looking mouth, bright red and round with big front teeth. His mom said it looked like something out of an early 90s candy commercial. Fischer wasn't alive during the early 90s, so he had to take her word for it.

Fortunately, it didn't do much, and hiding it from his classmates had been easy. When he felt that burning, itching feeling that preceded its growth every spring, he would keep his long sleeves until it went away, even though his friends at school were just starting to exchange their winter clothes for short-sleeved t-shirts and tank tops.

"Hives," he would say to his classmates.

"Oh," they would say, and they would back away.

"It's not contagious," he would remind them.

But they usually kept their distance for about a week anyway, just to be safe. Fischer was actually relieved by this, since temporary ostracism lessened the chance that they would discover his second mouth.

It was the spring of Fischer's twelfth year when his arm-mouth first spoke.

"Hey, hey!" it said—during math class, of all times.

"Fischer," his teacher said, "when we have a question in class, we raise our hand."

"It wasn't me, Mrs. Snodgrass," Fischer said.

Mrs. Snodgrass tightened her lips and turned back to the chalkboard.

"Hey, buddy!" said the mouth. "I'm hungry, man! When are you gonna feed me?"

"Shut *up*," Fischer whispered, and he clamped a hand over his arm. It let out a few more muffled syllables and stopped.

But it was too late. The teacher slammed her chalk down and whirled around. "I won't stand for this, young man. Go to the principal's office."

"It's not my fault!" he said, horrified. "It's. . . it's. . ."

His teacher waited with hands on hips, her mouth a thin straight line, but what could Fischer say? He couldn't tell her about the mouth. Even in the off chance that she believed him, then she and the whole class would know he was a freak. He was already getting some strange looks from the girl next to him.

He hung his head. "Yes, ma'am."

He gathered his things and walked out of the classroom, feeling everyone's eyes on his back, hoping his ears didn't look as burning red as they felt. He clamped his hand over his arm as he went.

As soon as the teacher's door closed behind him and he was alone in the hall, the mouth bit his hand.

"Ow!" Fischer said. "What'd you do that for?"

"I couldn't breathe," the mouth said. "Let's get some food, man."

"I can't," Fischer said. "I have to go to the principal's office. They'll know if I don't go."

"Ah, who cares? I'm hungry! I need some grub!"

"Why are you talking to me? You never used to talk."

"There's a first time for everything."

This made sense to Fischer. After all, his normal mouth had learned to talk when he was just a little kid. Now that he thought about it, he wondered why his arm-mouth had taken this long to start.

"Well, there's nowhere to go. Lunch was over two hours ago. The school isn't very close to town. What do you want me to do, walk five miles to a restaurant?"

"No way. Call a cab!"

The mouth said this a little too loud for Fischer's comfort. He shushed it and made sure he was alone in the hall before he continued.

"Where exactly do you think we are?" he whispered. "This is Augustus Valley, West Virginia. And we're not even in the town limits. There aren't any cabs here. We'd be lucky to see a car going by the school, even luckier if they'd pick us up."

"I'm feeling lucky, baby!" Fischer's arm said. "I'm feeling lucky, and what's more, I'm *starving*."

"No. I won't do it. Mom always told me it's dangerous to ride in cars I don't know."

The arm-mouth was quiet for a second, like it was thinking, or probably fuming. Even though the lips were closed, he could feel his arm-mouth clenching its teeth.

He started down the hall—still empty, thank God—toward the principal's office. As Fischer was about to check in with the secretary, his arm said to him, quietly, still through gritted teeth, "You think you're in trouble now? I can make things a lot worse for you. You know I can. I can make your life *hell*."

Fischer's arm-mouth stopped. The secretary had seen him by now, and she peered over the desk at him through thick glasses that made her eyes look like tiny black-eyed peas.

"I . . ." Fischer started. "I think I'm not feeling well. Can you call my mom?"

"I'll have the nurse—"

"No! No, please, just call my mom."

The secretary squinted at Fischer, something adults often did when they were trying to tell if he was lying. He thought of it as their Liar Vision, because it seemed like adults usually *could* detect when he was trying to pull a fast one. Some adults had their Liar Vision amped up too high, though, and would often default to seeing dishonesty in him even when there wasn't. The school secretary was this way.

However, he really *wasn't* feeling well, not at all. The secretary picked up the phone.

Even though his face still showed his discomfort, he felt the mouth underneath his sleeve spread to a wide grin.

The mouth was silent as Fischer's mother drove him home. He was glad; though his mom had known about the mouth his entire life, he was too embarrassed to tell her about the new symptom.

"What kind of sick is it, Fischer?" she asked. She took a hand from the steering wheel and set it on Fischer's forehead. "You don't feel feverish. Is your stomach bothering you?"

Fischer almost affirmed this, but then he realized that if he did, she wouldn't give him very much food, and he needed something to feed the mouth—and he was pretty hungry himself.

"It's my head."

"Aww, I'm sorry, baby. We'll get you some ibuprofen and let you get some rest. Just lay back until we get home. How's your arm feeling?"

"My arm? Oh, um. Normal. For this time of year. Actually, I think it might be going away early."

His mother's face brightened. "Well that's great! Maybe you're growing out of it!"

"Yeah, sure, maybe," Fischer said. He leaned the seat back and feigned sleepiness for the last few minutes of the drive to avoid further discussion.

Fischer and his mother lived by themselves on the fourth floor of the little apartment building on Main Street next to the train tracks that split the northern and southern halves of Augustus Valley. Whenever a train went by, Fischer liked to lean out his bedroom window and watch the iron serpent slither over the bridge and through town. The trains were less common each year, but he still often rested his elbows on the windowsill and watched the foamy Augustus River rage under the railroad trestle.

Back in his room, he watched the river through his window. His mother had sent him to bed with a plate of crackers and some water—"I'll let you know when it's supper-time, you just rest 'til then, sweetie," she had said as she closed the door—and of course his arm-mouth hadn't let him keep any of those crackers for himself. They were saltines, so neither could the arm-mouth spare Fischer any of the water—"It's dry as the Sahara in here!" it had said.

So Fischer gazed mournfully into the rapids, feeling very thirsty and sorry for himself.

Saturday morning greeted Fischer with bright rays through the window and smells of pancakes and bacon through the door. He sat up and rubbed his eyes. His arm yawned obnoxiously.

"Yowza—smell that breakfast," it said. "I'm getting all watery."

Fischer sighed and put a hand on his own rumbling stomach. It wasn't fair that his arm got to eat all the best food and leave him with little for himself.

Not this morning, he thought. *This morning I'll eat pancakes and bacon myself.* He crossed his arms.

"Ow!" he cried, and uncrossed them. A large, toothy indentation remained on his skin.

"Sorry, not sorry," the mouth said. "You were smothering me in there."

Fischer grumbled and left his room, the bacon's aroma pulling him forward.

"Hi, honey, are you feeling better?" his mother said. She set a sizzling skillet of bacon on the table next to a steaming plate of sourdough pancakes. "Do you want some eggs?"

Fischer nodded and sat. He forked three pancakes off the stack and plopped them down on his own plate, then he scooped three floppy pieces of dripping bacon next to them.

"Pss!" said his arm.

Not now, he thought. *Not with Mom here.*

"Pss!"

"What was that, Fish?" his mom said as she poured him a glass of milk.

"I um . . . I'll be right back. Need to pee."

"Sure, honey."

Fischer ran into the bathroom, furious. "*What?*" he said to his arm.

The mouth twisted in a scowl. "I'm hungry, dude. I was just going to make sure you were planning to save some for moi."

"I think you've had enough."

"I think *I'll* have the say-so in when I've had enough. Mister Bigshot, with the eyes and the nose and the ears, thinks he's got the right to bully me around! Well you're not going to starve me, Mister Eyes-and-Nose-and-Ears. I'm *hungry*. And I *will* eat. You just try and stop me and see what happens."

Fischer's heart fell and his stomach rumbled. He didn't need to see what would happen. He knew. It had been hard enough to hide this thing before it had learned to talk. It might soon learn to scream.

He went back to the breakfast table with his head down.

"Honey, are you sure you're all right?" his mother said.

"You know, Mom, I think maybe it's better if I take this to my room today."

Lines creased his mother's forehead. She ran a tender hand down his cheek while he kept his arms stiff and tight to his side. The mouth took a girth of shirt and skin into its teeth and clamped down. In turn, Fischer clamped his own teeth over his lower lip, to muffle the pain.

"Oh, my poor baby. Go on, I'll bring you your food."

He nodded and hurried—but not too fast, he was supposed to be sick—back to his room. He climbed into bed and hid himself under the covers.

His mother followed with a plate that held two pieces of bacon and one measly pancake. "You don't want to upset your stomach, dear."

He nodded, crestfallen. She stroked his cheek briefly and then left.

There was only enough food for one mouth, and Fischer cried as he watched the bacon and pancakes disappear under his forearm.

Not even a truly sick boy can stand imprisonment for long. Within a quarter hour of his arm's breakfast, he was already conjuring a plan to escape quarantine.

He looked out the window for any possible means of freedom. A rain gutter ran next to his window all the way to the ground below. He reached out and tugged on it as a preliminary test. A section of the gutter broke loose from the old building, and he let go in despair. Below him, the Augustus roared, indifferent to his plight.

"Listen," he said to his arm.

"I'm all ears!" said the mouth. It guffawed, and then: "Actually, I'm all mouth!" It continued laughing in brainless hilarity until Fischer clamped his hand over it.

"Shh," he said. "You have to be quiet." He removed his hand, and it remained silent. "I'm going to try and sneak out the front door. So you can't make any noise."

"Sure, sure, you got it, boss," the mouth said, and it grinned. "I could use a day on the town."

Fischer had never left the house without his mother's knowledge before, and he was surprised at how easy and thrilling it was. When he got a block from their apartment complex, he let out a sigh of relief.

"Yahoo!" his arm cried. "We're free, baby!"

Fischer looked around for anyone who might have heard. But it was Augustus Valley, and even on a sunny, blue-skied Saturday morning like this one, it was rare to see more than a handful of cars drive down Main Street over the course of a whole day. The only person Fischer saw was a bent old man walking a mangy dog a few blocks ahead, well out of hearing distance.

The novelty of Fischer's illicit freedom waned as the hour passed, but his hunger did not. He soon found himself in the gas station, standing in front of the rolling hotdog cooker. The shining, plump tubes of turning meat entranced him; the salty smell of hot cured beef and pork carried him to unearthly realms of pleasure and ache.

"Holy smokes!" said that all too familiar, grating voice, breaking Fischer's revelry. "I gotta have me one of them dogs!"

"Didn't you just eat?"

"That was like . . . well, a while ago. I'm dying here! You gotta get me a dog, man!"

"You all right over there, boy?" came the clerk's gruff voice. Fischer leaned his head out from behind the shelf of white sandwich bread hiding him from the register. "Just talking to myself."

The man nodded and went back to ogling the dirty magazine that he imagined he had cleverly concealed within a newspaper.

Fischer's attention went back to the hotdogs.

"Well?" said his arm.

He shook his head. "If anyone's going to be eating anything, it's me."

"Oh, you think so, do you?"

After another heavenly, hellish minute of watching the dogs turn over on their rollers, the mouth spoke again. "I'll make you a deal. You get us a dog. I won't make a scene, and I'll share half of it with you—not a bite more than half for either of us. Scout's honor."

Fischer sighed. He stuck his hands in his empty pockets. "I've got no money."

"Excuses, excuses."

Fischer was shocked that something that came from his own body could conceive of theft. Only *bad* kids stole, the ones that his mother always warned him not to hang around.

"Come on, kid," the mouth said. "We're both hungry."

The mouth was certainly right about that. And it had promised to share. . .

He poked some tongs in through the warm opening of the hotdog cooker, and the arm-mouth smiled.

"Feels good, don't it?" it said. "Feels *right*."

He snagged one and then stuffed it quickly into a bun. His heart was beating so strong, he was afraid the clerk would hear. His hands trembled as he squeezed zigzags of ketchup and mustard on the hotdog. He forgot the coleslaw and chili that was next to the heater; he just put the hotdog in a cardboard tray and then held it behind his back as he walked out of the store. The man never even looked up from his magazine.

He stepped out into the blinding sun and then broke into a full sprint for two blocks. Finally, he stopped, panting, hotdog in hand, stomach growling.

"All right, my man, give me that."

He held the hotdog back from his arm for a second.

"Only half, right?" he asked.

"Yeah, yeah."

He fed the dog to the arm. It devoured the first half in two bites, and before he realized what was happening, the whole thing was gone.

"Hey!" Fischer yelled.

The mouth's lips approximated a shrug. "Hey, it was good. I was hungry."

"You promised!"

The mouth only laughed. Tears stung the corners of Fischer's eyes. Something besides hunger now churned through his stomach: betrayal.

"You're gonna pay," he said to his arm. "I don't know how, but you're going to regret that."

"Ooh, I'm so scared," the mouth said. "You're the one who stole it, not me. Far as I'm concerned, you got what you deserved. What are you gonna do, kid?"

"I . . . I'm not going to feed you anything anymore, that's what I'm going to do! I'll starve us both before I listen to you again."

The mouth snarled. "You know I can make your life miserable. You really want anyone else finding out about me?"

Fischer gritted his teeth.

The mouth began to scream. "Thief!" it cried. "That boy is a thief!"

Fischer ran in a blind panic while the arm kept proclaiming his crime for all of Augustus Valley to hear. Windows opened, and women and men poked frowning faces down at the boy. He didn't make eye contact, he just ran, tears burning and blurring his vision. As he got closer to his house, he heard something besides the mouth, something louder. He looked past his house and saw the train on the other side of the bridge.

He stopped running and looked down at the screaming mouth, then at the whistling train. He scrunched his face in determination and then ran past his house to the train tracks.

When he got to where the tracks crossed the street, panting heavily, the train was almost across the bridge.

If he'd had any more time to consider what he was doing, he might never have done it. He lay down parallel to the rails on the street and stuck his arm out. The whistle moaned, and the train's brakes locked, but it was too late. A hundred tons of steel rolled over his arm and separated the limb and its mouth from the rest of his body. The mouth stopped yelling, and Fischer passed out.

Fischer awoke in a hospital bed. His mother stroked his forehead; there were tears on her face, but she smiled.

"Mom?" he said. He felt weak and sore, and a little dizzy.

"Fischer, what were you *thinking*? You shouldn't have been playing near the tracks."

"I . . . there was something . . . my arm. . ." Fischer tripped over his words, trying to figure out how best to explain what he had done.

"Shh, honey. You just rest. Oh, sweetie." She wiped her eyes. "We're so lucky. God bless the doctors. What a miracle."

"But Mom—"

"You just sit tight, Fish. I'll go get the doctor and let him know you're awake. I think he'll want to check on a few things."

His mother kissed his forehead and left the room.

Fischer took a deep breath. He was safe. He was alive. But he had put his mother through a nightmare of worry—he did feel guilty about that.

But it's over now, he thought, and he smiled. *It's finally over.*

His forearm itched, and he reached to scratch it with his other hand. His stomach went cold and twisted; his smile faded. His arm!

The doctors had reattached it! It was sore and scarred, but there it was. He flexed a fist back and forth. It still worked. Which meant...

The mouth was gone for now, but the spot where it had been itched furiously.

"No!" he shouted, and scratched the spot madly, leaving bright pink streaks on his pale skin. "No, no, no, no, no!"

The doctor rushed in. "What's wrong?"

"You should have left it off! You should have left me alone!"

"It's all right, boy," the doctor said, putting a hand on Fischer's shoulder. "We got you all back together. You don't have to worry. That arm isn't going anywhere."

Fischer lay his head back on the hospital pillow and cried. Just below his forearm's scratched skin, he felt curling lips and a twitch of laughter.

Timothy G. Huguenin writes horror from the dark Appalachian hollers of West Virginia. He is the author of the novels *Little One* and *When the Watcher Shakes*. You can find out more about him and his writing at http://tghuguenin.com/.

THE GIGGLE ROOM
By Nick Manzolillo

You'd think the word "pussyfart" would never fail to get a few laughs in the room, but The Showroom Live audience shrank back as if Chester Strauss were threatening to show them his taint. The sweat from his palms ran slick across the microphone and before he could get his bearings, the five-minute warning light began flickering from the back of the room like an SOS.

"Think on that one for a bit, you'll get it. I'm Chester Strauss, ladies and gentlemen, have a good night." The polite applause those Massachusetts morons gave him as he left the stage was as much of a participation trophy as it gets in the comedy world.

The comedian that went on before Chester, a black guy from Philly named Louie with a reputation for impersonations, slapped his back and whispered in his ear, "It happens to everybody, man," and then gave his full attention to the next bozo that stepped on stage. If it weren't for the fact that three other comedians (not to mention a waitress) told Chester the exact same thing all in the past two weeks at a handful of other clubs, he would feel better. As it is, even at reputable Boston joints like The Showroom Live, Chester only gets to go on for the marathon 4-7PM show, which means half the audience are a bunch of bored stiffs that don't drink, have nothing better to do on their day off and are too cheap to pay the cover charge for the real comedians that come on at 7:30. That's what almost every other standup was to Chuck, "real."

There was a chance he could get on stage for another gig across town at 11:30. A chance that would still result in him waiting two whole hours for barely five minutes of stage time, and that was only if nobody ran over their set; if at least half the audience decided to stay for the late show. Boston was no New York, and speaking of that rotten apple, even that city's shoddy no cover charge Improv clubs (if they could even be called that) would only give Chester one or two spots a week. The one time he stayed in the city his funds were nearly drained, even after crashing on a buddy's couch.

At some point, he knew he'd have to make his way to that damn city outside New England's grasp. All the other Boston comics who made it did their time there, from Louie C.K. to Bill Burr. It's a rite of passage, suffering during your early years and crashing on couches, living with three other dudes in a studio apartment in the middle of the worst neighborhood in Brooklyn. Chester heard every act there was, read all the autobiographies and watched every TV show about a comedian that kickstarted with Seinfeld. He was versed in comedy culture, and had even had a few intimate mentor/student pep talks with a few of the roaming big shots that still visited the smaller clubs to touch up on their act. Little had changed the fact that Chester sucked.

What's worth remembering about being terrible at the thing you lie awake all night dreaming about, is that, if you have the slightest bit of self-worth, you don't give up. You adopt the philosophy that with dedication, you'll become successful, even if it's not until your mid-forties. Chester, at twenty-eight, was comfortable with that idea. What haunted him was the question of whether or not he was even doing enough. Was he preforming at enough gigs? On the weekends he already drove three hours between sets at random, desolate clubs scattered from Providence, Rhode Island to Bar Harbor, Maine. He did everything from one night or annual bar gigs to amateur hour at the X-finity stadium before rock concerts. He even once did an education based set at a high school, but what was the marker for not trying hard enough to succeed? Was it not sleeping? Was it giving up on shit that made you feel alive like going to the occasional movie and playing a shit ton of games on your phone? If only the fucking crowd would laugh at least half the time, then Chester would know he was on his way.

He slouched across the bar and ordered a beer. Most comics can get at least three beers on the house, even if they bomb. At least that's how it works at the The Showroom Live. A cluster of three comics who hadn't yet preformed were on the opposite end of the bar, forming their own little trifecta of banter that would only be tainted by Chester's inclusion. Chester took a pull of his Narragansett and watched the cute wiggle of a waitress's butt. He could always find some way to keep his spirits up. He began writing a bit in his head, about how nice asses can cure depression, when somebody sat down next to him.

An older man with unkempt, gray hair, dotted stubble, and a leather jacket that looked like a lost relic of the 1970s took a seat beside him. "You're out of the hospital?" the bartender, a quiet guy who never talked much, said to the stranger, pouring him a rum and coke.

"I never bothered goin'," the man, presumably a comic, said, looking Chester up and down before downing half his drink. "Not a good night, huh?" the man said, and even though the stranger was looking right at him, it took Chester a moment to realize he was being spoken to.

"Not the worst," Chester said, trying to play it cool.

"I heard you while I was having my smoke in the backroom. Man, you weren't good," the stranger grinned, and Chester got it, comedians don't exactly say nice things to one another, *but fuck this guy*, he thought. He began to guzzle his beer, so he could leave and sulk in some corner of the city on his own.

"I know of a way to help, if you're interested. If you don't mind me saying, you've got the look, kid. You've got the gravitas, as they say. You sound like you could be a hit, but you don't sound like a hit, yeah?"

"I'm good, thanks, I've got coaches," Chester said, trying to end the conversation.

It was still early, most comedians with any sense of professionalism wouldn't drink before the later shows unless they needed a confidence booster or were good-for-nothing drunks. This was beginning to seem like the latter.

"I'm Rocko Dunham," the man said, and something began to click for Chester. Rocko Dunham, he'd hear that name before.

"I've got a secret and I'm at a point where I'm willing to share it. You're the lucky sucker, and I mean that in more ways than one. Sucker, who's sitting on the barstool next to me," Rocko said, and the word "sucker" had all sorts of nasty emphasis to it that made Chester want to break his bottle over the guy's head. Rocko was a big time New Englander who went on an impressive streak in the nineties, transitioning from standup to co-starring in tons of comedy movies. He hadn't made headlines in a decade, and Chester assumed that was because he both had writer's block and was filthy rich to the point that he didn't need to bother finding work anymore.

"You're not going to make me suck your dick, are ya?" Chester said, only it didn't come out funny.

"No, kid, you're not sucking any dick tonight. Or any ever again. Unless you want to, that is," Rocko said.

"I'm all set," Chester eyed the bartender to see if he was listening, but he was talking to the waitress with the cute butt.

"Do you know who I am?" Rocko asked, and Chester figured it out. Rocko talking to him was some kind of prank. The security camera in the corner of the room was probably going to be uploaded to some ball-busting website.

"Yeah, I mean, I grew up watching your stuff, man. Just, I didn't expect you to be here," Chester said, and Rocko laughed. First pleasant thing Chester had heard all night, despite Rocko's voice sounding like it'd gone through a cigar/rum woodchipper cocktail.

"Then you ought to trust me when I tell you I know of a place that can make you big time. No cost, you just gotta know somebody."

"Man, this isn't even, like, a good prank, huh?" Chester asked, and so much for getting air time. He'd talked with big shots before, meeting Rocko did almost nothing for him. Actually, it pissed him off. Fuck these people, kicking him while he's down.

Rocko laughed, splashing more booze down his throat. "This aint' a joke. If it was, you'd die laughing," and that almost sounded like a threat. "There's a spot, upstate New York. 'Longside the Hudson, bout three hours outside the city. Who the fuck knows how long from here. There's a club only comedians are allowed to go into. I'm not going to tell you the name until you see it yourself, and if you tell anybody the address, you'll know what being blacklisted really means in the industry of the world, kid. You won't even be able to get a job pumping gas down in the boonies."

"Dude, I'm not falling for it. Why the fuck would I drive hours away for you to bust my balls? Joke's over," Chester slammed the rest of his beer and made to leave, but Rocko grabbed his arm.

"I'll come with you," he said, his lips parted to reveal yellowed teeth that apparently having boatloads of money wasn't enough to fix. "Could take my rig, assuming you walked here," he said, and he assumed correctly.

"I don't believe this. . ." Chester said, and Rocko laughed again.

"Don't. Wait and see. Then you'll believe," he clapped Chester's arm, finished the rest of his drink, and then threw a hundred-dollar bill on the bar.

"Here's hoping you only fuck my ass after you murder me in the woods," Chester said, swinging his arm enthusiastically. Rocko didn't laugh, again, and this time Chester was sure he was at least a little bit funny.

One of the comedians clustered in the trio raised an eyebrow at them and said hello to Rocko, to which Rocko responded with a grizzled, "Fuck you," as he led Chester out into the early November evening.

Rocko's rig was a dark red '69 Corvette with a newly redone interior and a modern engine. "You're driving," Rocko said, and Chester, who owned a Nissan that might as well have been from '69 as well, was all too happy to go along with that. Six to eight-hour drive be damned. "Head to New York," Rocko told him before shutting his eyes. He didn't open them when Chester asked what radio station to play, and for the next four hours until he got the next set of instructions, he wasn't sure if Rocko was asleep or not.

There was next to no talking for the rest of the trip, not that Chester didn't try. "Working on any new movies?" nothing. "Still doing standup?" nothing. Chester debated asking Rocko if he was a fat sellout, but the guy was letting him drive a Corvette, as old as it was. It was a nice car, if a little cramped. The engine's roar made Chester remember all the dreams he'd had of conquering the world.

With the full scope of night bringing the shadows to life around them, Rocko told Chester to turn onto a woodsy road where he continued on for thirty minutes. Chester asked, "You sure you're not moonlighting as an axe murderer?" Rocko smiled as if, somehow, he was still drunk after the last six hours. Chester did leave him alone in the car when he got gas a few times and snagged a Subway sandwich.

"Pull up to yer left," he said, and as far as Chester could see he'd turn the Corvette into a nexus of pine trees if he listened to Rocko.

"Where?" he asked, glancing at Rocko and driving right past a dirt road.

"There," Rocko pressed his face to his window, frowning as Chester pulled a U-turn down the hidden road. It was narrow, but the Corvette was almost perfectly small enough as they kicked down the road, a small cloud of dust trailing after them in the fading glow of the headlights.

It was more or less what Chester figured, a bar in the middle of nowhere. Its namesake, The Workshop, was painted McDonald's style in red and white on an old wooden sign hanging above the front entrance. The place was well lit, with a dozen cars in the gravel parking lot. Typical of a comedy club, there were no neon beer signs or any real charm at all.

Chester pulled out his phone, and of course there was no signal. It was a little after two in the morning. Sure, it was New York and all, but he was in the middle of hickville, and he wondered what kind of hickville club stayed open so late.

Chester tried to ignore the sense of alarm that began to crawl over him when Rocko took the Corvette keys from him. Who did the other cars belong to? A couple were nice but for the most part, they were average. Like anybody else that reads around on the internet, he'd heard of groups of celebrities forming a sort of illuminati amongst one another. Could this be it? The group of people who really run show business?

"Am I, like, going to perform?" Chester asked, following Rocko to the entrance.

"You're going to keep your eyes wide open and your mouth shut. When you take a seat, you fold your hands and press your knees together. You don't ask questions when we get inside. You do, and you drove out here for nothing. And I'll leave you out here. We ain't friends. Remember that," Rocko said. This was going to be some kind of hazing ritual, Chester was sure of it.

"Long as nobody touches me," Chester said.

"Naw, it wouldn't come to that. You cry though, you look away and back down and ignore what's coming, and you won't have what it takes. Maybe I'll buy you a bus ticket back to New England, in that case," Rocko said. There was no doorknob on the front door, a massive wooden panel that Rocko leaned against with a grunt before it finally began to budge open. Despite the number of cars outside implying that there were a fair number of people within The Workshop, there was only silence when Chester followed Rocko inside. Nobody jumped out and said surprise. There wasn't so much as the sound of an ass impatiently fidgeting in a seat.

Where Chester expected there to be a main bar room or lobby with a ticket booth, there was only a long hallway. The wooden planks on the walls pulsed with life, as if The Workshop were the opposite of a log cabin. There was a musty, damp smell to the air, as if the place absorbed the rain and never quite let it go.

Rocko leaned against a wall and Chester realized his eyes were closed, squeezed tight as if Rocko were trying to blink something away. "Go on to the last room on your right. Take a seat. It'll begin shortly after. Remember what I said. When it starts, hold your eyes open if you got to."

Chester eyed the angle of the hallway. There were lights overhead, but they seemed to get dimmer further down the hallway. "Man, what's down there?"

"I get it," Rocko said. "You're not much of a believer, are you? You think skill is enough sometimes. You think you don't need luck, you make your own, yeah? Forget all that. Believe. Not in God, but the divine, yeah? Think of it like this. You're Achilles, the great warrior from *The Illiad*, right? Remember how he became such a badass? His mother dipped him in that magic river that made him invincible, yeah? Well, I'm your fuckin' mother, and if you show me you got balls, I'm not going to miss the back of your ankle, either." Rocko sounded like he did in the old movies Chester used to watch, and that was convincing enough for him. He walked as quickly as he could to the last room on the right and entered.

The moment he twisted that too-cool-to-the-touch doorknob, Chester felt as though he were about to say the wrong thing to a girl he was out on a date with for the first time. The minute the door creaked open, he couldn't turn back. The only thing in the room was a single folding chair, illuminated by what looked like a stage light from somewhere in the shadowy depths of the ceiling. Thinking what he had to do next was obvious, Chester walked over and took a seat.

The room was bigger than he first assumed. Aside from the wall with the door he entered, the other corners of the room were dark and capable of hiding anything. Chester looked over his shoulder, and even though he expected it, he almost leapt out of his seat when somebody walked out of the shadows. It was just some random middle-aged asshole who looked like he was going bald. Other people stepped free from the shadows as Chester hyperventilated in the moldy stench of the room.

"Holy shit," Chester said, unable to keep himself silent. A dozen people formed a circle around him, giving him about five feet in diameter. Others continued to emerge from the corners of the room. Finally, it dawned on Chester that what he thought were shadows were actually a curtain that acted as the walls of the room. It's almost as if he was backstage. Shoulder to shoulder, thirty people silently surrounded Chester, looking at him as if he was the last bite of some meal they didn't want to waste but were in no rush to eat.

A random woman wearing a scarf was the first to laugh. It came out as a chuckle, and then burped up through her belly. She was joined by the balding man that Chester first saw, and like a jumping virus the laughter swept through the crowd that had Chester boxed in. For a moment, he thought of the crowd he'd heard cheering on the better acts he'd seen, but this was different. They weren't pointing at him while they laughed, but they might as well had been.

The faces of Chester's audience crinkled up as the guttural barking ripped through their open mouths. The ha-ha's began to melt together as the crowd reached a bizarre level of synchrony that went beyond any concert Chester had ever been to. They were mutated hyenas, both wounded and feasting at the same time in the middle of the desert. An echo began in the room, and Chester realized that the circle of people around him had grown. His estimate of how many people there were was drowned out by the sound pulsing against the sides of his head. What was thirty people could easily have been a hundred, if not a whole stadium full. The floorboards beneath Chester's feet began to vibrate, followed by the chair and his very bones.

"Stop it!" Chester yelled, and he couldn't control himself. He instantly wondered if he had failed, if the strange optical illusion of mad laughter had already gotten to him. The laughter was literally vibrating him, though, that was no illusion. His bones were moving, his skin was rippling. He raised a hand to his head and his hair was blowing. His teeth began to chatter, and his eyes were watering. The faces around him began to melt together and he started to wonder what the people around him were thinking. What was so funny? How could they force out laughter like that?

Time slipped. Five minutes could easily have been fifty. Chester began to panic, wondering how the people around him were capable of breathing. They would die, they would laugh themselves to death if they kept it up any longer!

"Please!" Chester said, or, at least, he tried to say. He couldn't hear himself talk, and it didn't feel like he said a word with vowels. It didn't feel like he spoke at all, rather, if felt like he let out a low chuckle. The laughter around him was moving his stomach. Pulsing the blood through his veins. His heart could have stopped, and the laughter would have kept it pulsing. The neurons in his brain were dancing. The faces around Chester weren't happy.

Chester met his reflections in the eyes of those around him, and something started to happen. The crowd, as vast and infinite as it was, began to grow. Like a funhouse mirror, his audience sprouted up another three to four feet, their heads narrowing and becoming cone-shaped. Their limbs and fingers lengthening like noodles. The only thing that didn't change was the laughter, as Chester felt himself shrinking in his chair.

Time continued dripping, and Chester realized he was laughing too, but he still couldn't hear his voice. He couldn't hear his words or, hell, he couldn't even hear his thoughts. His ideas. He felt the panic and confusion dabbled with fear that surrounded the strange circumstances he found himself in, but he couldn't hear the small stuff. There was only laughter, and in between each primitive and guttural sound, there was a sequence. A code that began to illuminate itself at the forefront of Chester's vision like a glowing strand of DNA. He wouldn't be the same, is the thing. If he shut his eyes, he began to realize that he could make the laughter stop. He could blink, and the room would become empty. He would be free to leave, to go back to normal.

Fighting back the tears, Chester followed the strands of glowing logic that had replaced the faces of his audience. The laughter began to break down. He could hear each voice. Each individual bark. Facing him as they were, each person was laughing at something different, even though they saw the same thing and were in on the same joke. The elongated people around Chester began to lift their fingers and point, and they elongated further still. Needles dug into Chester's skin, and he welcomed them. He understood. That's all it takes, to be great. *To hit them where it counts. To find their Achilles heel.*

At some point, Chester realized he was sitting alone in a room laughing by himself. The door to the hallway was open. Nothing moved behind the curtains. Chester shot to his feet, and the chair tipped over behind him. He didn't look back. He didn't peer into The Workshop's other rooms.

Outside, in the Corvette, Rocko was asleep in the passenger seat. It was daylight, late morning. Chester didn't question anything. He was hungry, and exhausted, but he got behind the wheel where the keys were already resting in the ignition, and he drove and drove back to Boston. Rocko didn't wake up, and Chester didn't try to wake him up. He parked right outside The Showroom Live, then closed for the daylight hours, and he left Rocko to sleep in his car.

Back in his shrimpy apartment, he began to plan out his act. He didn't do anything special. He tried not to think about that room in The Workshop. When he performed the material the next night, the crowd applauded and hollered for so long that he thought he was back in the room. *The Giggle Room.* He zoned out, and the next guy following his set had to push him off stage and make an off-handed remark about how he was a deer in headlights.

Two weeks later, Rocko was found dead in his home outside of LA from an evident overdose. Another three weeks, and Chester was the opening act at The Showroom Live. When he asked every-body how they thought he improved, they only laughed. Maybe they said something else, but that's all he could hear. When the agents and managers and showrunners and producers eventually came his way, he found that he couldn't really hear them, either. They would laugh, and laugh, telling him he was funny, and all Chester could do was nod.

Nick Manzolillo's writing has appeared in over forty publications including *Wicked Haunted: An Anthology of the New England Horror Writers*, *Grievous Angel*, *Thuglit*, *Red Room Magazine*, and the *Tales To Terrify* podcast. He has an MFA in Creative and Professional Writing from Western Connecticut State University. By day he works as a content specialist for TopBuzz, a news app. He lives in Manhattan and spends the little free time he has growing a beard.

THE FINAL ALTAR
By G.D. Watry

The altar was carved from ruddy sandstone by the Befallen.

Silas straightened the damp blanket on his father's shoulders and ushered the raggedy man over the final step. His father shivered from cold and exhaustion. The man was a bone bag leaking mucus and whimpers. Silas turned around, checking back on the day's journey.

The spiral staircase wrapped around the mesa. Below, the valley lay bleeding darkness. The last licks of sunlight flittered on the horizon, spitting and spurting their final throes before the day's death. A thin strip of highway snaked across the desert, all the way from the mesa's base to the collapsed city in the distance.

The gargantuan man behind Silas coughed and raised his eyebrows. They'd all been walking for hours and stopping here, right at the veil's threshold, was like a tease. The man was nearly two heads taller than Silas. In his tattooed arms, he carried a small woman, her body like a deflated balloon with taped sticks for limbs. A teal bandana held her feathery, silver hair still in the desert wind. Hardened wrinkles creased her coal eyebrows, and her dry tongue wriggled like an earthworm between the gaps of her rotten tooth smile.

Silas nodded an apology and continued to the stone pews.

Columnar cacti stood like silent sentinels around the open-air cathedral's perimeter. The rows were filled with the city's elderly and their guides, usually the closest living relative.

Silas guided his father to their assigned seats among the congregation and looked at the sky.

It darkened, and darkened, and darkened.

Like the extinguished lights of the city, the universe beyond the third planet winked out of existence in the Aftermath. The blue of day was still blue, but the night was jet and starless.

Silas couldn't make sense of it. He'd rationalized that the sunlight was so intense it blotted out any semblance of the Befallen's actions beyond the Earth's atmosphere. The night, however, revealed secrets.

Silas' father bent over. He reached for his shoes' Velcro straps with trembling hands.

Silas stopped his father. "We're not home," he said.

His father looked at him with the vacant stare of an infant. The man hadn't spoken in days. The silence setting in like always before the Shuttering.

A metallic whir buzzed from above, and the Cosmic Gaze opened.

The synthetic eye peeled back like a satin skin fashioned from collagen fiber. The eye's surface rippled like a stone-disturbed pond.

"We are wrapped in your embrace," the congregation said in unison.

And then it started.

The ground trembled beneath them.

People cried out, their voices dwarfed by thundering quakes. Silas felt his father's stiff fingers wrap around his hand. The base of the altar cracked. Something murmured beneath the earth, the buzzing drones of a machine-learning hive.

Cables unspooled from the altar's maw, slithered through the air like synchronized swimmers, searching for their homeports.

Silas shut his eyes.

His father's grip didn't tighten. It only lightened and dropped. Loud electric pulses, like static heartbeats, filled Silas' ears.

The Befallen had vanquished death, now nothing more than Transference.

As the bodies dropped, dust returned to earth, Silas wondered where else the soul would rest if not with the Machine.

G.D. Watry is a writer living in California. His previous work has appeared in *Pantheon Magazine*, *OCCULUM*, *The Sirens Call*, *Shotgun Honey* and *The Molotov Cocktail*, among other publications. He can be found on Twitter @GDWatry.

SIGHT UNSEEN
By Leah Bond and Peter Rawlik

I can see you there. Looking back at me. Watching me. You think you are hidden, that the mirrored glass provides for you some kind of refuge. But I can see you. You're as trapped here as I am. Do you understand that? Do you understand any of what has happened? You want to understand. Shall I tell you? I doubt the telling will change anything, but you need to hear it, to understand, and I—I need to tell it.

My name and place of origin have no bearing on this tale. What is relevant is that I suffer from a rare disorder. My affliction is degenerative and held at bay through the daily application of a pharmacological suspension directly to the eyes. Two drops of Xavier's Solution in each eye counteracts the loss of transmission in my optic nerves and allows me near perfect vision. Without my medication my sight would become blurry and then cloudy, until within a matter of days I would be almost completely blind.

I relate this bit of information to you because I think it is a key factor in what happened over the last few days, and might provide an explanation for the ghastly events that befell the Family Sprague. I had been invited to spend the winter holidays with them by Andrew, a classmate whom I had become friendly with. We had been together three years, studying aquatic ecology, and there was some suggestion that we might be more than just friends. As my own parents had tragically passed away, and my sister found my supposed decadent lifestyle rather repugnant, I readily agreed to Andrew's invitation.

It was through the cruelty of fate that our paths had even managed to cross, and a stroke of kindness that such a solid foundation of our fellowship had been forged.

We had been paired up in a basic level laboratory exercise, and he happened to be seated next to me when the uniformed officer arrived to inform me of my parents' tragic accident the night previous. Andrew had dealt with a similar incident years before, with his own father, and somehow continued to stay by my side throughout the varied phases of my grief. I have a feeling his comfort towards me had healing effects for him, too. Throughout the resulting whirlwind of emotions and events, I immersed myself in my studies. Paired with Andrew, I somehow managed to bury my pain and not only succeed, but excel.

It was just days ago that he and I undertook the journey cross-country, with the last significant leg being completed by train from Boston to Arkham where Andrew's sister, Helena, an unassuming waif of a woman, was waiting to drive us out of town. We drove northwest along the Miskatonic River. I observed the vista of the small city slowly transform into suburbia, then farmland, and finally into sad overgrown fields that bordered on the shore of a vast, gray lake. It was not actually a lake, Andrew informed me, but rather an artificial reservoir that dated back to the early part of the twentieth century. Once the area had been prime land for agriculture, but a blight had destroyed the crops and the local farmers had spiraled into abject poverty. Too poor to fight the disease that had afflicted their land and too proud to sell their ancestral plots, the residents of the area had fallen one by one to that most vicious of modern terrors—taxes.

Slowly but surely the county and state acquired the acreage in the small valley that adjoined the Miskatonic River, and when none were left to object, they laid the earthwork, and the pipes and the pumps and flooded the land, making sure that Arkham would always have sufficient drinking water. Except, thirty years later the city turned to groundwater sources instead, and left the reservoir in place only for emergencies and to provide water for a local bottling company.

As the pastoral scenery continued to roll along, I sunk deeper into the back seat of Helena's aging car. She and Andrew had much to discuss, and although she remained fairly silent, the range of their discourse was wide and varied, abridging years into simple statements, mere words. Back to our first meeting and the sudden entrance of that officer. My resulting meltdown. I pretended to listen to the muted music piped through my earbuds, staring mutely at the landscape as it passed beyond the window. How Andrew and I managed to change our rooms first semester and then continued to cohabitate for the next three years. He rattled off a few flings here and there, aimless trysts, little more, while I tried to remain stoic on the subject.

My own family situation had decayed beyond repair. My sister had wanted me to return "home" to settle affairs regarding the parental estate, but why? I had realized there was no longer a home to return to, not anymore. Given our disagreements on my degenerate lifestyle, any ties were ultimately cut. This journey with Andrew had become a new homecoming for me. In a sense, the Spragues were now family to me, family I had chosen, sight unseen, through Andrew.

The house, a rambling edifice in the craftsman style dating back to the mid-twentieth century, sat on a ridge between the reservoir and the Miskatonic River itself. Family history said it was built as a residence for the first pump operator and his wife, but Andrew readily admitted that there was no evidence to support that claim. As we pulled into the driveway I could see that the home was surrounded by a dense, overgrown forest of fir trees to the north, while the sides hosted now-fallow vegetable gardens. It was in its way a typical rural Middle American scene, a stark contrast to the urban blight that Andrew and I endured outside the rented apartment we shared in Philadelphia. In the late afternoon light, with the sun setting across the reservoir, the Sprague family home seemed as inviting as any I had ever visited.

The mild winter meant that the cold was tolerable and the grounds free from any snow or ice. The earth was hardened though, and gave a satisfying crunch as Andrew and I trudged about. We fell into a routine those first few days. We were roused at seven by Mrs. Sprague banging about in the kitchen. Breakfast was scrambled eggs with melted provolone, bacon that was equally crunchy and chewy, and home fried potatoes seasoned with onions and peppers. Her coffee was dark, rich and savory with a hint of hazelnut and some other seasoning. In fact, all of her food held an underlying complexity of flavors that included components that I could not identify. Mrs. Sprague put it down to fresh ingredients, as opposed to the overly salted bits of grease and canned vegetables that were our staple at Wissa-hickon University. I disagreed, but did not pursue the issue, for as I sat there at the table I felt a sense of welcoming and family, a sense of just *belonging* that was hard to deny.

After breakfast, we would wander about the property and Andrew would point out the sights, and we would smoke our ciga-rettes. It was a habit that Mrs. Sprague did not allow in the house. Consequently, we smoked in the forest, but were wary of this as the entire property appeared dry as any tinder box, and one stray, smol-dering butt could easily set the whole place ablaze. The surrounding environs seemed in need of a healthy measure of fire management, for as with most natural areas the usual cycle of burning had been suppressed, and vast amounts of fuel had accumulated across the forest floor, with only a few well-worn paths snaking their way through the undergrowth.

Those paths through the woods to the north of the house were a fine way to spend our mornings; though I must admit I was a little uneasy at first. There was something entirely unwholesome about those trees. They grew so strangely, their branches reach-ing—straining—not for the sky, but rather toward the river. It was as if the trees themselves yearned to be free of the soils they rooted in. But it was not merely the orientation of the branches, but their very structure as well. Their bark was gray, almost ashen, as were the lonely dead leaves that still clung to their parent's skeletal branches. Though through both I thought perhaps there were some hidden memory of color, a vein or scintilla of the prismatic that still lingered amongst the dull colors of decay. I observed that same effect in the flesh of the myriad species of fungus and lichens that had col-onized the litter that covered the forest floor. There was it seemed a great paucity of color to the forest that bordered the Sprague home, save for that ever-present ashy gray, and the queer lingering sense of something forgotten or lost, something that lurked just beyond perception.

So distracted was I by the preternatural dullness of the wood it took me a full day to realize that color was not all that was missing. As we trudged along those paths the only sounds that reached our ears were those that came from our own boots. I ex-pected for the place to be still, but it was more than that. There should have been the rustling of leaves and underbrush as rabbits, woodchucks and other small game moved about. There should have been some birds, there are species that do not migrate, but none were present, not even owls. There should have at least been owls.

But there was nothing, no birds, no small game, no animal life at all. There was merely the gray expanse of litter, and the unwholesome and bent, knuckled trees that strained to be free. We should have not been in that place, it was abnormal in its way, but we went there daily and wandered as if we had nothing to fear, as if we belonged there. The only sounds were our heavy footsteps, the metallic clank of my silver-plated lighter, and our voices lost amongst the trees.

We returned home for lunch on a daily basis, and slaked our hunger with soup and sandwiches prepared by Mrs. Sprague and Helena. Helena, like her mother, was a slight woman, attractive in her own way, though a bit taciturn in my opinion. I had a sneaking suspicion that the whole point of the trip was for Andrew to introduce me to her. I tried to be pleasant, but unlike her brother the girl could not hold a conversation and refused to join us on our morning walks, though Andrew said she was an avid hiker. Surprisingly, she was an excellent card player and we spent the afternoons playing hearts in front of the fire.

"Well played," I offered after a run of particularly fine hands. "I'll need to take a hike to walk off that beating."

"Those woods may as well be the back of my hand," she muttered, "We could head out after dinner if you'd like." Taken aback, I nodded my agreement.

Dinners in the Sprague household were not extravagant feasts, but rather comfortable gatherings consisting of either chicken or lamb from the farm on the other side of the wood. The vegetables came from the family root cellar, which was well-stocked from what Mrs. Sprague called "her award-winning country garden," though when she said this Helena would roll her eyes to indicate that the older woman was exaggerating. After the evening meal, Andrew and I sat in front of the fire with snifters of brandy, a particularly fine vintage that Mr. Sprague had purchased in quantity almost a decade ago. The bottles had sat almost untouched, a kind of memorial to the old man who had unexpectedly died before the liquor had even been delivered. His tragic loss all those years ago became our gain.

After lifting our glasses to the late Mr. Sprague a second time, Andrew motioned towards Helena, who asked from the kitchen, "You ready?" as she walked toward the rear of the house. Of course I wasn't. With a furrowed brow, I shook my head, gesturing to the window behind me and the fading skies beyond. She reassured me over her shoulder, "Come on, you'll live," and shut the back door of the house behind her.

Feeling awkwardly committed, I bade Andrew a hasty fare-well and grabbed my coat from the chair over which it had been draped. I slipped on my boots and stepped outside, shrugging into the warm leather jacket as the cold air hit my face. Slightly inebri-ated, I clambered up the path toward the forest and made my best attempt to catch up to my companion. As my footfalls shifted from the crunch of gravel to the crisp rustle of leaves, I was thankful the branched arms of those trees were not reaching for me. I could hear the fall of her step in the distance ahead. That being said, her stride was much shorter than mine, and I could easily outpace her, but she knew these woods, and unlike myself she wasn't half-drunk. With time however, my rhythm soon matched hers and we reached a small clearing together.

It took a moment for my eyes to adjust to the absence of il-lumination, the half-waxed phase of the moon provided ample light to navigate, but it wasn't the level of urban light pollution I was ac-customed to. I leaned against the bare trunk of a tree and gazed up at the night sky as the remaining blanket of dusk fell beneath the horizon.

"I don't imagine you have nights like this in Philadelphia, huh?" Helena suggested, stepping away into the glade.

"Not really," I resumed my skyward stare, in awe of the pan-oramic display as it continued to reveal itself.

"I like it better at night," she continued. She didn't seem to care about these misshapen trees, with their gnarled and arthritic twisting arms. Helena wove her hands among one of them, grasped it firmly and swung herself around the trunk to stand beside me. If I didn't know any better, I could have sworn the pair moved in unison, and complete silence.

"I never was one to focus on book studies, like Drew was. Or still is. I don't know what all he's been up to. It's been almost five years, after all. You both get on well. He's had nothing but good things to say about you. He's been talking about possibly getting on up at M.U., in their Ecology Department or something. It'd be a haul to Arkham every day if he intended to stay here. About an hour each way, if he went that route, if not longer." She went on. "I'm happy for him, it's good that at least one of us has done something with our lives."

"What makes you think that, Helena? That you haven't done anything with your life?"

"My place is here with Mom. Since Dad passed . . ." She seemed suddenly guarded and changed the subject. "I always have enjoyed being out here, under the sky. Looking at the stars and the clouds." She sighed, and I could hear a touch of sadness in her voice. Then she took a deep breath, looked into my eyes, and committed herself to something. "When Dad was alive, Drew generally stuck his face in some book and I always ran around out here. You've got to admit, this is a pretty substantial backyard."

I grunted agreement.

"Mom thought I was something of a tomboy and I'll not disagree, I still am." She then lifted a side of her jacket to reveal a flask she'd filled from the coffers. Helena drew a quaff and offered it in my direction. I was all too eager to comply. Fortified by drink she began to talk and walk weaving away from the paths to which Andrew and I had trod, heading west, toward the reservoir. Her monologue continued, about how Andrew became her parents' pride, how she began to feel secondary. Her nights out in the forest evolved into an event of great anticipation and greater secrecy, one that continued for years. Then, during a dry spell, she recalled her parents talking over dinner about how the lack of rainfall had depleted the water table and the county had been draining the reservoir to supplement supplies to Arkham. As the reservoir continued to drain, previously submerged areas had started to resurface, and much to the dismay of public safety officials, some adventurous individuals had begun to wander out into the muddy flats. Some were just exploring, others visited their ancestral homes. The chance of injury was terribly high, and the activity was officially condemned at several public meetings. Signs were posted, and wildlife officers routinely patrolled the area. Trespassers were to be arrested and fined heavily.

Of course, Helena had to see this! That next morning, she feigned being sick, making sure Andrew and her parents weren't around to curiously stick their noses in and muck up her plans. She "borrowed" Mr. Sprague's neglected hip waders. He had been so excited when they moved here, about the fishing that was sure to be had. But they remained tucked away in the garage ever since his first and final unfruitful excursion. They would be busy until later that evening with Andrew, some award ceremony with school. She would have to be quick. Over time, it seemed Dad had lost interest in most of what happened at home. She remembered her father telling her she had passed the age of magic being real, not believing in Santa or the Easter Bunny anymore, and that she had left that 'fun' age behind, he would just have to get used to not having her as his little girl anymore.

After that talk, she noticed the evenings had become less interactive. Everyone began to develop their own separate habits and schedules. It seemed the family became less unified. His absence from the dinner table, from the home in general, became a much more frequent occurrence.

Was it somehow her fault?

Was it her own lack of embracing 'fun' that dampened the spirits of those around her? This question remained unanswered, despite Mrs. Sprague's insistence that this was most certainly not the case, in the one instance that she did share her thoughts. Even though her mother had pinky sworn she wouldn't tell, her and dad's heated discussion—*he even said the D word, and they were different people now?!*—travelled through the ventilation ducts, clear enough that this betrayal of trust was evident to all. She fell asleep to the sound of weeping, and some of those tears were her own.

Her father's waders were much too big, so she had to roll their tops down across her much smaller thighs to make them fit. Even then her feet were too small to fill her father's boots, and she had to use old newspapers to fill the toes. It made walking difficult, and she felt like some gigantic rubber balloon, quite ridiculous, really, but she was thrilled beyond caring. It wasn't the standard night time hike she was accustomed to, and that made it all the more exciting.

The reservoir lay beyond the forest to the north and west of the house, and she had become familiar enough with the paths that led there, she had nearly trod them to the point of muscle memory. Through the broken gate which the locals used as a short-cut to the highway and then across the graveled access road at the corner, she made sure the recent patrols were not within earshot. Down the ravine, and she'd popped out of sight from across the road. She looked back at the slope and knew that getting back was an obstacle she'd have to address later.

After she left the road behind and slipped through a small stand of dead ash, the drained reservoir finally began to reveal itself. A blasted greyish crater, pristine in that its surface remained untouched, a concave and blank bowl of sediment settled peacefully with not one mark or track to disrupt the surface of this newly discovered alien landscape. If anyone had already been there, it would have been easy for her to tell. She realized once she entered that crater, it would be that much easier for someone to find her.

Onward she plodded, thankful for those giant, oversized boots that kept her dry. The day was long yet, and there was a trace of low clouds in the western sky. "Strat-ohh-kyoom-yooolus," Helena broke the silence, let her mouth form that word, long and foreign to her still. Ms. Mason had told them all about the different kinds of clouds in Nature Studies. Those lofty, distant puffs were given a name, and through the action of her having named them, they didn't seem so far away at all. Her plodding trek through the vast, colorless landscape continued.

Many of the remaining structures had collapsed, like ruins of some sort of ancient civilization. On rare occasion, an identifiable edifice could be seen, a past construct that proudly stood in defiance of the circumstances which befell it. Malevolent monoliths they were, and she the spiteful sprite that sprinted among them. Within the ruined lands she saw an area where the discoloration and grey were almost radiant, a lone lump that rested in a clearing of dead tree trunks, all of which seemed to lean sharply away from what appeared to be a steep indentation on a small mound. The trees having been trapped by their roots and able to run no farther, fell flat to the ground in an arcing circle around what appeared to once have been a well, the kind you threw pennies in to make wishes.

She didn't have any pennies. She would have looked for a pebble instead, but the surface of everything was coated with a thick, creamy layer of muddy sludge. The surface of all, save the interior lining of that lone well, bored deep into the earth. One of her barrettes would work! *A wish won't work unless it feels like a sacrifice,* she remembered hearing once. *What am I willing to give up? What do I have to lose?* Helena pulled the shiny clip from her scalp, and stepped up to the circular formation, in the center of what seemed to be those toppled, aged trees—that well. Now it was *her* well, and damned if she didn't come all this way . . . if she wasn't going to make a wish.

Solemnly gripped, the tangles of hair removed, the barrette was pressed into her forehead as she leaned into it, and muttered a wish, a soft prayer for her family, brother and school, then her Father. ". . . and please Dad stay with us," she finished, and dropped the barrette into the well. It fell for some time before a muted rattle was emitted as it came to a final rest in the darkness below.

Helena felt one lone, cold raindrop hit the back of her neck, which shattered the hypnotic fixation that had enveloped her while she had gazed into the pit. The skies darkened, and those stratocumulus clouds must have heard her call, however faint, because here they were, and much greater in number. She turned back, seeing her ragged trail, fading back to the edge, and knew that she was much farther than she had ever intended to be. She had to make haste before the rain came to wash away those dotted tracks, and in turn, the waters that would inevitably rise. How much time had she wasted with that childish ceremony?

By the time Helena followed her tracks back to the edge of the reservoir, the rain had begun to fall, steady and sure. As she stepped onto the firmer shoreline it became a downpour. She knew her parents would be quite upset, and viciously so. Breathing deeply, she faced mounting that ravine in the pelting rain. As she scrambled up the steep embankment the rain washed her clean, and soaked her cold. She knew she was most likely a sight to behold, and what a sight she must have been, bundled up in those oversized waders! At least the skies had darkened quite a bit, providing her with additional cover. With some struggle, she managed to claw her way up that ravine, avoided the rusted corrugated drainage pipes that punched their way out of that wall of exposed earth, below the access road she'd crossed earlier and prepared to cross again.

After a great deal of struggle, she finally rose from the side of the ravine, and gripped the guardrail that circled the drop she had risen from. She was certain she looked an absolute mess, the waders had begun to take on water, she could feel the rivulets as they ran down her calves, and formed pools around her frigid toes. She was over halfway home and it was just the gate left, easy to cross. She had done it before and would do it again.

Halfway across the road however, she was met with a pair of headlights, honking and swerving. She dove into the surrounding brush and went still. She could hear the engine of the patrol car—or was it a truck?—and waited for someone to get out and come after her. After a minute or so, when no pursuer was obvious, she set off at a dead run—she didn't want to be caught like this! She knew how mad her parents would be.

Helena began to remove the waders and their excess strappings on the way to the back door. Her mother's car was in the driveway, and the woman burst into the garage as she tried to hang the hip waders back on their peg. Andrew had been standing behind her as she launched into an epic diatribe about being responsible, and how she had been worried sick. She did get cleaned up and ready for bed, accompanied by the berating voice of their mother, who was absolutely livid. So angry was she that it was hours later that she finally noticed Mr. Sprague, who had driven to the school straight from the office, had not yet returned.

It wasn't until two weeks later that Mr. Sprague's truck, and subsequently Mr. Sprague, was discovered. In an attempt to save time in his rush to get home, he had taken that access road, and in the process lost control of his truck, careened off the edge and into the muddy waters of the reservoir. The windshield had broken in the process. Storm water pumped in from the river had filled the truck and sunk it deep into the gray mud below. It wasn't until a game warden noticed the errant tire marks through the bank that he rolled down the window and was assaulted by the smell of rot. He followed the marks down to the water and found the truck. With a new perspective, the trail of crushed vegetation was easily seen. Mr. Sprague had crawled through the wreckage and then up the levee, he almost made it up to the road, coming to rest in an irrigation ditch, partially covered with a strip of rusting corrugated metal. They had found his bloated body where he had died, cold, hurt and alone.

Helena blamed herself, of course. It was all her fault. He had swerved to miss hitting her. But her wish had come true. On the mantle in the living room, the remains of Mr. Sprague sat in a decorative urn, watching his wife and daughter, and his son and his misguided friend, drink his brandy. He had stayed with the family after all.

It was all so morbidly sad. As she fell into my arms and moaned in anguish, I suspected that Helena had never told anyone else about this. She had been just a child, but in her mind, she was responsible for her own father's death. No wonder she never had any motivation to do something with her life. She had dedicated herself to her mother and Andrew as a kind of penance. As we walked back to the house I kept my arm around her, and I suspected that it was a kindness she had never before been shown.

It was later the next evening that the sequence of events that led to the tragedy began, and they began with that brandy. Andrew and I had imbibed a modicum of the supply and had nearly emptied an entire bottle. Rather than return the bottle to the cabinet Andrew vowed to finish it off, but he had woefully underestimated the volume remaining. Instead of us both having just a little more, we each had almost an entire extra snifter. An hour later than normal, we stumbled upstairs to our rooms and I fell into a deep alcohol-induced sleep.

It was the morning after, distracted by the remnants of the night before that a critical error was made. I was roused at seven as normal, and went through my morning ritual including dressing, washing my face, brushing my teeth and administering the medicated drops into my eyes. Afterwards, I sat on the bed trying to gather up my energy and make my way downstairs. I closed my eyes, telling myself I just needed a moment's rest, but instead I nodded off. I woke just a quarter hour later, but my mouth was pasty and dry. I went back to the sink and used my toothbrush again, trying to wipe the filth from my tongue. Then I took the small bottle of drops and once more administered Xavier's Solution to my eyes. It was a reflex. A simple course of habit that I didn't even notice until it was too late. I realized my mistake immediately, but beyond a bit of cursing I paid it no heed.

And yet I could feel the changes a double dose was having on me.

At first, I attributed my discomfort to the excesses of the night before. My vision was blurry, light and sound hurt my brain, my hands trembled, and even my tongue felt fat in the back of my throat. It was a typical hangover, or so I told myself. But as I came down the stairs I began to feel very ill. My stomach turned, and I nearly doubled over in pain. Instead of going into the kitchen I grabbed my coat and bolted out the door. I needed fresh air, I told myself.

As if that would have given me some relief.

Stumbling down the walkway I kept my head down, the jacket pulled tight over my ears. The air was cool and it felt good against my face, but the sun hurt my eyes. I don't know why I wandered into the woods, force of habit I suppose, but I did, and there in the shade of those twisted trees I finally lifted my gaze from the frozen earth and looked about me with eyes open wide and perhaps for the first time able to see the truth. With my first look at the wood that morning I fell to my knees, crumpled like a ragdoll, and wretched onto the forest floor.

What I could only glimpse before was now plain to see. That hidden, lurking scintilla of the prismatic was now exposed, and I realized the truth of things. The forest, the strange trees and underbrush that comprised it, the mushrooms and lichens that populated the forest floor, even the fallen branches and leaves that littered the place were all alive, pulsating with an alien color that could have no name. Yet as I sat there almost entranced by the extra-terrene I came to realize that it was more than just a color, but rather a kind of pigment, not unlike those found in plants and algae. This pigment was however infinitely more efficient than those used by earthly vegetation, and instead of reflecting back a portion of the spectrum and appearing as green, or orange, or yellow, or red, it absorbed nearly all electromagnetic radiation leaving only the barest trace of color—the ashy gray that dominated the forest.

That it was some sort of invasive species, an alien parasitic infection was clear. What was worse was that it seemed not to be bound by the boundaries of any single organism, or species, or even kingdom. The entirety of the forest and all of its components were not only infected, but formed together a kind of super interconnected organism. I could see entire networks of unworldly veins and arteries that stretched between trees and through the brush and the dead leaves and even the organisms of decay. It was all connected, all one thing, and I could see it stretching for acres. And I knew that it was malevolent.

I do not know how I knew this, I just did. I could feel it in the darkest recesses of my mind. This thing, this unnatural color that permeated everything in the forest was anathema to human life. In time—years, perhaps even decades—it would spread further and further, infiltrating our entire ecosystem, until humanity itself was infected by its unnatural pigment.

I knew all this, and I knew that it was at that moment at its most vulnerable. I took my lighter out and set fire to the nearest pile of dry paper-like leaves. They went up like tinder, and the flames spread like nothing I had ever seen. They ran along the ground, igniting the litter and accumulated detritus. In moments the fire had spread in all directions and was even racing through the underbrush and up those gray tree trunks and their queerly shaped branches.

I ran from the wood, not so much from the spreading wildfire, but from the response that it had engendered in the parasitic color. The thing was fleeing, moving out of the inflamed portions and concentrating itself in the vegetation that had yet to be scorched. It was like a wave, like an unearthly aurora roiling through that wilderness, through the trees, and the bushes and even the forest floor itself.

It fled the fire, and like myself, had no direction to run but towards the Sprague family home.

I burst through that door yelling for my friend and his family. It was my intention to evacuate them from the home before the fire reached the backyard. Their voices were panicked and full of confusion. They were in the kitchen, cleaning up after the morning meal. I ran to them, screaming into that room, my heart pounding, my lungs aching, but I never said a word. The ability to speak simply left me.

All the colors were wrong. The faces of my friends, my ersatz family, Andrew, Helena, their mother, were horribly colored, like a television in which the tint had failed. The normal soft progression from shade to shade was now strikingly exaggerated and it made the Sprague family caricatures of their true selves, clowns in riotous pastels that seemed to writhe about on their faces as I watched. It was a revolting, repellent thing to witness and I was unable to endure. Like a madman I turned from the room and collapsed in the den, crawling in front of the fireplace, drawing comfort from the purifying flame that dwelt there.

I knew what had to be done.

With the poker I pulled the flaming logs out of the hearth and let them roll out onto the floor, setting fire to the rug and nearby curtains. Andrew tried to stop me, but the poker swung in my hands and embedded in his skull with a satisfying crack. He went down on the floor and into the flames and never got up again. As I came into the kitchen Mrs. Sprague didn't even scream as I ended her life.

Helena just looked at me with big, watery eyes. She didn't understand what was happening. Her mouth opened, and my name spilled out from between her lips. But at the same time something horrible crawled across her face and I swung my weapon. She died, and the infection that was hidden inside her like a malignant cancer, died with her.

With my hosts dead and the flames licking at the house itself, I stood outside and watched with my now preternatural empowered eyes as the alien color drew itself out of the forest, and the house, and the grass, and the leaves and all the dead, rotting litter. It concentrated itself in a few great pools of refuge on the edge of everything. But it was too big and the remaining volumes too small to hold it. It was like a hermit crab that had outgrown its shell trying to find refuge in one that was obviously too small. It struggled and in its own way groaned in anguish, a mournful shift in color, like an octopus signaling its mood. The small oaks that dotted the edge of the forest seemed to swell with the infestation, pulsing and stretching till their seams were ready to burst.

And then they did. They burst forth in unison, exploding out of their host like a mass of multi-chromatic pus, streaming across the open air, exposing itself to the environment, to the atmosphere of our planet, perhaps for the first time in decades. It was an insubstantial thing, a gossamer of corruption and eerie light. Vulnerable it seemed to react almost immediately as if it were oxidizing, interacting with the chemicals and compounds that made up our world, and decaying because of it. It combusted in a violent display of energy that left a thin powdery ash in its wake. A trail of gray powder fell from the sky like a corrupting snowfall, blanketing the yard in alien ash. In mere moments the invasive pigment was gone, wiped out of existence by one of the simplest chemical reactions, against which it had no true defense. As the last of it burned away I myself finally succumbed to the strain and fell to the ground, and watched with a kind of psychotic glee.

The state police carried me away from the scene. They let a paramedic look me over before they drove me off to the local station and then threw me in this room. They've left me in here for more than an hour now. Nothing but a chair, a table, a pad of paper, and a pencil. There is the mirror as well, a vast plate of polished glass through which, I assume, they can see me. But I can see myself as well. And I know that I am not alone in this room.

I know you're there. I can see you. I can see you there. Looking back at me. Watching me. You think you are hidden, that the mirrored glass provides for you some place to hide. But I can see you. I can see you squirming, unsettled in your own way. I don't know when it happened. Was it a slow possession that began the moment I came to the Sprague House? Was it while Andrew and I walked in the woods? Was it after I set them ablaze? Was it while I sat there dumbfounded watching the world burn?

When was it exactly that you fled inside me, contaminated me with your scintillating, alien prismatic? I see you there. Lurking behind my own eyes. You think you've found a haven, a refuge from the destruction I've inflicted. You assume that I wouldn't notice you. An excellent move, and with anybody else it might have worked. Self-preservation is a powerful motivation, but I know what happens to animals that are parasitized. I've seen them fall into the downward spiral of playing host to an ever-increasing load of infection. I know the final outcome. It isn't pretty.

Sooner or later the guards will slip up. Self-immolation is a horrible way to die, but it will be worth it. I find the whole idea somehow calming. Almost Zen-like.

We'll burn together, I promise you that.

When not brewing up adult beverages, playing with strange soundmaking devices, or immersing herself in Patient Advocacy, **Leah Bond** can be found penning various reviews and performing interviews for the fellows over at legendsoftabletop.com.

A prior tale of hers can be found in the Summer 2016 issue of *Mantid Magazine.*

Peter Rawlik is the author of more than fifty short stories, the novels *Reanimators, The Weird Company,* and *Reanimatrix,* and *The Peaslee Papers,* a chronicle of the distant past, the present, and the far future. As editor he has produced *The Legacy of the Reanimator* and the forthcoming *Chromatic Court.* His short story *Revenge of the Reanimator* was nominated for a New Pulp Award. He is a regular member of the *Lovecraft Ezine Podcast* which in 2016 won the This is Horror Non-Fiction Podcast of the year award. He is a frequent contributor to the *New York Review of Science Fiction.*

THE ATLANTOW
By MarieAnn C. Raguso

Lisette Abendscheim should have been excited to celebrate her father's fortieth birthday, but she was distraught. She hated the manor. She hated the land in which the manor stood. The soil was soaked in a bloody past which she wouldn't quite grasp until later that night. It was chilly that day and Lisette was bundled up. Her head began to spin a little as she approached the tree. She blamed the thick layers for overheating her.

Frederick, her father, was sick and she feared the worst for her own health. She couldn't afford to get sick now, she had to take care of her father. It was a strange reunion. Lisette deeply loved her father, even though he had shipped her off to a boarding school in the city soon after his wife's death.

The leaves on the trees were enchanted with yellow and orange hues. Some lush green pine trees sprinkled in along the property's backdrop. It should have been a place of untainted splendor, but it wasn't. One tree stood out amongst the foliage, a ten-foot Roundleaf Dogwood tree that sat in the center of the front yard. Lisette didn't want to remember the tree. It was a bleak reminder of misery, particularly, her mother's death.

What attracted her to the tree was the wind, which shook a branch with one purple leaf hanging from it. The tree appeared to be in full bloom as if it was spring. The rounded leaves were waxy and thick in texture, and should have had vein scars coursing throughout them. They should have been an assortment of dying colors, too. But, in all cases, they were not normal as they never changed from green and lively.

The leaves waved her over as the wind danced through the alley of trees that led to the front door. They seemed to sparkle through the sun's setting light. Lisette swore she saw the faces of people in the outlines of the leaves' veins. Her heart stopped as she thought she recognized one of the faces—her mother. The purple leaf had yet to develop a face.

"Lisette, get away from *her*!" Lisette's father yelled from the doorway. He limped around with a wooden crutch under his right arm. Lisette felt his green eyes had been transformed into two grey pebbles. Grey pebbles—like the ones that lined the walkway that led up to the manor house.

The manor house was made of large quarry stones and looked foreboding. It almost imitated a dismal mausoleum, but with turrets on both sides and a wide wooden front door painted black. As it was, Lisette hadn't set foot in the manor since her mother's death eleven years ago. The autumn hues gave the manor an eerie, haunting glow. It stood out from the rest of the landscape. The black windows reflected the foliage in them like a mirror.

His voice shook Lisette out of her trance. The dizziness had vanished, along with the faces in the leaves. She shuddered at the thought. She ran into her father's arms. "You shouldn't be out of bed, father," she scolded, all the while looking back at the ominous tree. Frederick reached out to grab the door, losing his balance at first. Lisette pulled at him, placing his arm behind her shoulders, helping him to close the front door. She assisted him upstairs, shooing off maids and butlers who tried to intervene.

It was not unusual for the family to find dead birds beneath the tree. As she had witnessed the day she arrived. Once eaten, the pale teal drupes on the tree would kill them within moments. Squirrels avoided the tree and wouldn't even bury their acorns in proximity to it. "Even butterflies and bumblebees wouldn't dare go near that evil *tree*," Frederick mumbled, ending with a rough cough as they ascended the grand stairwell.

They got to Frederick's room and Lisette sat him down on the bed. She disregarded what her eyes had just witnessed in the leaves. She insisted, "But it is *just* a simple deciduous tree, father. Trees hold no power over man."

Frederick looked at his daughter with grave concern. "In some sense, you are right. But no, my precious child. It is an unholy abomination. It is the Atlantow!" She had heard of the Atlantow in her childhood. It was some kind of great evil, like the Devil, though Lisette was not fully convinced.

She hushed him just as a butler crept into the room to assist Frederick with his nightly preparations. He didn't want his daughter to leave his side. At this point in his life, he didn't care if he was made ready for bed or not, but he had to abide Victorian social customs. Lisette left the room as custom declared. She didn't see the tear stream down his left cheek as she walked down the hall to her bedroom.

It was a presence like no other. A living, breathing tree, more like an insidious creature with hundreds of talons reaching out to grab ahold of its prey. Lisette recalled as a child, even horses would act strangely around it. The day her mother died was an example of the strange draw the tree—*or presence*, had over the Abendscheims. When her mother returned home after visiting a dress maker in the village, she was unable to steer her horse clear of the tree's path. It had appeared out of nowhere. It had not been there when Lisette's mother left that morning. The horse startled and thrust her mother off and onto the cold hard ground. She became quite ill after that, just as her mother and her mother's mother had before her. This mysterious illness ultimately claimed her life three days later on her birthday and in her sleep.

The tree seemed to be watching Lisette through the window. Frederick randomly coughed in his sleep, tossed and turned. She stood at the window holding the drape open and glared at the portentous Roundleaf Dogwood tree. She had to let it know she was standing guard over her father, just as she had done for the previous night and the night before that. Try as she may, she couldn't help but feed into the mythology.

It took her a few moments to pull herself away from the window. It was as though she was entranced by its glowing leaves in the moonlight. She walked over to the lounge chair that sat by her father's bedside. Frederick lay there looking helpless and grim. His usually pink flesh was pallid. His lungs heaved, and he struggled to retain air.

How could he believe such a myth? She thought she had seen her mother's face in a leaf, but tried to chalk it up to grief and worry about her father's condition. A diary sat on Frederick's nightstand. Lisette wanted to know more, *so what better place to look than in a diary?* With slight hesitation, she picked it up and began to read. The latest entry was dated by Frederick that very day. The earliest was from his father, Lisette's grandfather. After each entry, a date of death and details in regard to the death, were inscribed.

She placed the diary back on the nightstand. Then, her eyes narrowed to a bookshelf where Frederick kept the other family diaries. She wearily meandered over to it. She yawned, but shook it off. It was close to the witching hour.

There were about forty leather-bound, handmade diaries in order by year. Each was different in length and width. Lisette grabbed a tattered diary from the left side. It was the first in the Abendscheim series.

The first few pages had been written by Enrich Abendscheim, the first child of her namesake, born in the New World. Enrich wrote about the betrayal that the family had brought upon a local Mahican tribe. In the year of 1681, Arellene and Hans Fritz (his parents), claimed that the tribe had killed Arellene's unborn child with black magic, when in fact, the baby had been a stillborn. This wasn't hard for the local settlers to believe, as it was common knowledge then that the Mahican worshipped the goddess of the land—the Mother Goddess.

Ngutte Keesog, a Mahican youth, had aided the family for nearly a decade after they arrived in the New World. He helped the Abendscheims to learn where to fish, how to plant, what to eat and not eat. His tribe even helped in building the family's first home, at the time a log cabin. The Mahicans even fed the family in order for them to survive through the severe Hudson Valley winters. The Abendscheims were not as grateful or humble as they portrayed to the tribe. What they were really drawn to was the Mahican's land. Hans Fritz and Arellene plotted after she gave birth a stillborn. They convinced their fellow settlers that the Mahicans sacrificed the infant in order to appease the Devil.

It was decided and kept secret between the villagers and the family. At first thaw, having survived the harsh winter, the settlers gathered and slaughtered the Mahican tribe. Some Mahicans were burned at the stake, some were hung from tall trees and others were killed with swords and daggers while they slept.

In Ngutte Keesog's dying breath, he vowed that the Mother Goddess would avenge this people. The curse held true as that night the Atlantow appeared in the Abendscheim's yard. The land in which the Mahican had once run free, was now the property of the Abend-scheims. Shortly after the slaughter, Arellene took ill for a solid two weeks before her birthday, breathing her last breath on the day she should have been thirty-two years old. Nearly six months later, Hans Fritz also took ill under mysterious circumstances. He too died around his birthday, though it was his fortieth.

When Enrich had passed, his sister, Eliza wrote in the diary. For over two hundred years, each one of Lisette's ancestors had written in the diaries—a now, seemingly looming tradition.

A week before Enrich's death, Eliza sought out the guidance of an Iroquois tribe. They were quite reluctant to help her. Eliza wrote, *I realize now—the Atlantow is real—real as the Devil! The Iroquois sent me wayward with one piece of hope—the Atlantow cannot claim a soul on the expected night, so long as the soul is guarded. Nor, can it move in the presence of others, except by wind. Enrich is dead for I failed to stay on guard. . . There is no hope for us. God save our—*. Her entry ended with her death date filled in by her husband.

Lisette read from diary to diary, though not in their entirety. She couldn't believe she had never read them before. She froze when she came upon her great-grandmother, Lorelei's, diary. Lorelei had the only diary that stood by itself, though her date of death was documented by another on the final page. She had died before Lisette was born, but she had always heard stories about her. During the War of 1812, Lorelei had written about the Atlantow. It read:

The Atlantow appeared on the first day of the war—upon my mother's death. All in our family will perish due to the erroneous actions of our ancestors and their greed for land.—Yes, our transgression is most certainly 'greed,' of which we have no refuge from the Devil's claim to our flesh and souls.—The Atlantow is said to be a fury of vengeance, that chose the form of such a lovely Roundleaf Dogwood tree. It is enchanting and inviting, but deadly, like all things in black magic tend to be.

This morning, I found my father dead at 40 years. My mother had died the same way at 32 years. My parents were the same ages as all the those who have perished before them—32 for the women and 40 for the men. We are cursed forever more by the omen of this tree, or rather this entity—brought on by the evils our family released. If I had known the Devil was betrothed to the Abendscheims, I would have never said—'I do.'

Underneath the entry, Lorelei documented the deaths of her four older brothers (Jonathon, Lewis, Samuel II, Jaqueline), an older sister (Alva) and three older cousins (Constance, Lena and Samuel

III). The last entry written by Lorelei read, *Heed these words and enjoy life, as mine will end tonight, and yours will end soon.*

The family cut down hundreds of sacred trees for beams, firewood, and for crafting the pages of their diaries. The Abendscheims bought slaves to quarry and build their manor house, which was built in the late-eighteenth century. They defiled the land of the Mahican's Mother Goddess and the Atlantow was a reminder of this. The Atlantow was a reminder of betrayal. Like the Venus Flytrap to its prey, the Atlantow was a reminder of the inevitable death that drew the family in only to devour them.

Two hours had passed, and a pile of diaries surrounded Lisette on the floor. She was encircled by them. She flipped back and forth between diaries. Her palms became sweaty and her breathing was constricted. The more she read, the more her heart raced, and her head spun. It was as if she was stuck in an ethereal purgatory. She was determined to stay awake throughout the night—to stand guard over Frederick's soul. More so, she was ready to do whatever it took to keep her father alive, especially after she had read one of her first-cousins' entries. *When the purple leaves fall, all who are ill will plunge into the arms of eternal darkness.* She wasn't sure there was anything she could do, except to stay awake.

There was enough testimony to convince her; the tree was in fact the Atlantow. However, there had yet to be a mention of a death being witnessed. If Lisette could stay awake, she knew her father would survive the night. She now believed, that she was guarding over Frederick's very soul. After all, this was night three for her. Death was three-days late for Frederick. *Perhaps it wouldn't come for him?* she thought. But, the tree's luminescent glow in the moonlight begged to differ.

It was true what her ancestors had written. At certain ages, all those in the Abendscheim bloodline would die after a series of unexplained and incurable ailments hit them. The ailments would hinder them from acting erratic or fighting back, and took them away from indulging in daily pleasures. In some cases, like in her mother's case, Abendscheims were known to defecate themselves at the moment of death.

Often times, the ailments would appear two weeks before a suspected person's death. It took two weeks for Arellene to die from a mysterious illness, which began the day following the slaughter of the Mahicans. She began to experience cold sweats, a loss of appetite, fever and cold. It worsened over two weeks with her coughing up blood and unable to hold her bowels. She died on what should have been her thirty-second birthday by collapsing to the floor. Her eldest, Enrich, found her.

Only six months later, Hans Fritz nearly two weeks before his fortieth also contracted a mysterious illness and died the same way, except in his sleep. Since it was Arellene's lie that damned the Abendscheims, it would be the women who would always pay the penalty for greed and betrayal first—just like Eve and Adam.

For the last two hundred years, the Atlantow was a beacon of death for the family. Lisette read several stories of attempts to destroy it, but to no avail. Lorelei's warning was well warranted—the Atlantow was a destructive and evil force out for retribution. The Atlantow was what her church referred to as the "Devil." And, according to the diary, the Devil had claimed every member of her ancestry, including her mother. Lisette remembered her father tried to burn the tree to the ground when she was a child, but an odious wind kept blowing the torch out. She had forgotten all about it, until tonight.

She went back to the diary with Frederick's entries and read about her mother. *She's dead*—a tear drop obstructed a few of the words— *the Atlantow took her. I did everything those savages told us to do—only to my chagrin—none of it worked. I was downstairs for only a moment. Two minutes at the most! Cursed be! When I returned to our bedroom, leaves shrouded the floor, the window was open and my dear wife—dead. It was as if the tree had crept in itself to claim her soul.*

It was the first closure Lisette truly had about her mother. Her heart was pounding in her throat with the disturbing information. She was engrossed in the diaries and couldn't pull herself away, until she had to tend to the fireplace. She glared at the flames as she poked the logs around. It seemed like an absurd idea. *Could the Devil really be possessing a dogwood tree? Was the curse real or was it just coincidental?* Questions conjured more fear that sent shivers down her spine and rose goosebumps across her skin.

She wasn't sure what to believe, or rather, she didn't want to believe a macabre thing like this was possible. She went back to the nightstand and picked up the diary in which her father had written. It was a looming heirloom that she hoped to not have to write in for many years to come. She sauntered backs to the lounge chair. Lisette made herself comfortable and began to read Frederick's fears. She recollected the leaf that appeared to have her mother's face embedded into its veins. It had to be true. The Atlantow was tangible and it was a ghoulish power waiting to pounce.

Sometime during the night, Lisette had fallen asleep in the lounge chair. She thought she heard something scratching at the second-story window. But, it could have been a dream. The flames in the fireplace still glimmered with life, but were dying fast. She awoke, looking around. For a moment, she forgot where she was and realized she had fallen asleep. Without another thought, she scrambled to her feet. There before her, scattered in a path from the window to the bed, were brown, decayed leaves.

Her knees became weak and she nearly fainted. Lisette had read about what had happened to her mother only a few hours prior. And now, it had come to pass again. Lisette hurried over to the window to see where the tree was. It was closer to the front doorway. Her muscles grew weak and she felt an electric shock of realization go through her bones.

A single purple leaf fell from the tree as if on cue. Almost as though the tree was waiting for her to look at it, as if to say, *he's mine now*. The thick roots of the tree had risen out of the ground, as if they were legs. Lisette turned from the window and ran to her father. She began to shake him vulgarly, "Father! Father! Wake up, father!" It was useless, she knew he was dead. The Atlantow had claimed another life.

Some kind of madness grabbed ahold of her, she couldn't take it anymore. She raced through the manor, down the stairs, out the front door and outside to confront the spirit. The Atlantow seemed to stare straight through her for a moment, before fading into oblivion. It would surely return for her in eleven more years.

Lisette returned to her father's room where the butler stood before a spilled tray. He was in shock, but Lisette could no longer be. She took the diary and found a pencil from a nearby drawer to document his death. The event had made her bitterly yearn for her husband and her newborn son—who she never had the chance to tell her father about. He never asked her about her personal life. She was very much ready to return to them in the city. At least with them, she wasn't alone.

MarieAnn C. Raguso is from Valhalla, NY. She is a freelance writer and an MFA Student at Manhattanville College. She graduated with her Bachelor's in Anthropology and Sociology and conducted extensive ethnographic fieldwork in death rites. Her fascination with horror began when she was a kid with H.P. Lovecraft and 1960s Gothic Romance novels. Raguso now writes fiction while working her way through her MFA Program. She has been a guest speaker at the "StandUP for Women" [June 2015] and has presented two separate nonfiction pieces at Manhattanville College [April/December 2017]. She is also a veteran and a Purple Heart Recipient.

THE WALLPAPER MAN
By Caleb Stephens

We moved in a year ago. A month after Mom died. Just me and Dad and Piper and an old, salt-rusted Victorian with big dormer windows and a swooping front porch. It's not much to look at, really. A faded-blue clapboard construction fronted by a yellow-piss lawn and a view of the Safeway parking lot across the street. Not exactly what I'd had in mind when Dad told me we were moving to the coast. He'd said he needed to get away from her. Or from the memory of her, anyways. Something like that. Some bullshit line about missing her too much.

"Nick," he'd say with the nicotine lines sprinting away from the corners of his mouth. "She haunts me. Every night she haunts me, I can feel her in the room when I close my eyes. It's not good for me here no more. Or for you and your sister for that matter. We need a fresh start somewhere else."

But I knew it wasn't a fresh start he needed. No, he wanted to run. I could see it in his nervous, washed-out eyes every time we went to the store, darting this way and that, looking for the *I know what you did* looks. The tight smiles with the curt nods. The poisoned glances. And at home, the trash cans boiling over with empty vodka bottles and crumpled-up cartons of Camel Lights, the floors coated in dust—no one to clean them up anymore.

So one day in late October, he pulled up in front of my school with a U-Haul tacked to the back of our rusted-out '98 Chevy Silverado and we left. No warning. No time for goodbyes. Just a quick, "Get in, kid. I found us a place up the coast. A good place. A place we can get right again."

Piper cried the entire way. And me, well, I just bit my tongue.

The fear always starts in my toes when he speaks. A sinister prickle that blooms through my feet and curls up my legs like a swarm of hatchling spiders in search of a meal. Some writhing, webbed-over treat to devour.

"I can helps you. I can makes it all go away."

His voice is brittle and flutters through the air of my room like a wisp of acrid smoke.

"Will it gives it to me? Will it gives me the pain?"

I shudder in my bed and pull the sheets higher, close my eyes and hope to snuff it out, to drown it in the black void of my dreams; anything to make it stop, to make it go away. But I know better.

The Wallpaper Man never stops until I answer.

Sometimes, when I feel brave, I try to tune him out. I think about things like Piper's smile when I tell her my stupid knock-knock jokes. It's crooked-perfect, with a little gap between the incisors that lights up the room when she laughs. I think about Mom. About how she smelled like lavender when she hugged me. I miss those hugs. A *lot*. When those things don't work, when I'm too afraid to think about anything else, I focus on the fear. The color of it: black. *Definitely* black. Its consistency: thick, like Ragu. Its taste: a bitter copper like when I bite my lip—like how I imagine battery acid would taste.

It doesn't work.

Nothing does, really.

Nothing but answering him.

The Wallpaper Man is used to kids who can run.

Me, I have no use for legs.

The ALS took them six months ago.

Most people are nice enough when they see me. I mean, sure, they stare a little too long and nod a little too hard when they say hello, but they mean well. And the women. Oh man, do they drive me nuts with those big, fake plastic smiles and the way they talk to me. Like I'm dumb or something. Like I'm a two-year old. I'm not. I'm sixteen. I just look young.

The men, well, they mostly ignore me.

But whatever. I can't say I blame them. Who wants to spend time talking to death warmed over in a wheelchair? I sure as hell wouldn't. I mean, I can't even stand to look at myself in the mirror. I try not to. I know how I look. The right side of my face droops like a stroke victim, the muscles frozen in place and not quite working right, the other half compensating with a strange twitch when I talk, like I've stuffed my mouth full of sour candy. I have eyes that are encased in sharp sockets and my mouse-brown hair sprouts from my head in weird directions that don't quite make sense no matter how hard I try to smooth it down.

And the pain. It's my entire existence. Cramps that go on forever. Muscle spasms and skin sores on my legs. Joints that lock up like rusted old latches.

Despite this, like I said, most people are nice.

Everyone except Roger Elliot.

The bathroom door bangs open, and, even before he speaks, I know it's him. "Hey! Look who we have here. It's Nicky Twitch!"

"Leave me alone, Roger," I mutter into the floor.

Before I have a chance to brace myself, he's behind me, whipping my wheelchair around, sending the contents of my catheter bag all over my lap. The smell of ammonia stings my nostrils and I frantically wipe at it with a nearby paper towel, hope to soak it up before it sets into my jeans.

"Hey, someone needs to cheer—" The corners of his mouth tick up into an evil grin. "Oh, my God. Did you piss yourself? You did, *didn't* you?" He barks out a laugh that tells me something bad is coming. "That's *so* disgusting. Wait till everyone hears about this. Pissing your pants! What a baby."

He spouts a few more jags of laughter and stomps out of the bathroom, leaving me alone with my urine-stained lap.

Roger has everything.

Perfect bone structure. A strong jawline already sprouting stubble. Broad shoulders. Girls chasing him everywhere he goes. He even drives a red Dodge Charger that his lawyer father gave him on his birthday.

He still has his mother. One who loves him. It's not fair.

He's everything I want to be.

And everything I hate.

A ray of moonlight cuts through the blinds and washes over the yellowed wallpaper of my room. Over the Wallpaper Man: ten-inch serrated fingers fall past a set of disjointed knees. Angular shoulder blades. Bones that slope sharp into a razor-blade neck. His skull is long and segmented and punctuated by a jaw that curls inward, bones crackling, when he speaks. Ridged eye sockets bulge from either side of his head and shift when he moves. Four eyes in all. It's like something from one of those *Alien* movies, but so much worse because I can't see *all* of him. I'm forced to imagine the details. Forced to picture the true horror that lies beneath the wallpaper. The slick, black rows of teeth that sometimes flicker against it when he speaks. The skin I imagine to be thick and pocked and reptilian.

"Has it brought me the names? Has it brought me my three? Gives them to me and I will takes the pain, yesh?"

The wallpaper ripples as he glides through it like oil, his joints working in a sick, unnatural fashion as he moves. I think of an arthritic centipede. My stomach sours at the sight. The putrid-sweet odor of his breath washes over me as he nears, his foul exhalations awaiting my response. Night—after—night the same question: *Will I give him his gifts? Will I give him his three?* And night—after—night I croak out a wet-gurgle *no*, my voice a weak, dry breeze. Baby vomit. I don't want him to hurt anyone. But tonight, something's different. Tonight, something cold boils through my blood at the prospect of having to face another day with Roger Elliot in it.

Without thinking, I whisper his name.

I half-expect to see Roger sitting at his desk the next morning, slouched down jock-style in his chair. Maybe it was all a dream. Maybe I'm just losing my mind talking to empty walls. But as I roll past, his desk sits wonderfully empty. The sight of it fills me with relief. I can breathe. No looking over my shoulder. For today at least. And it only gets better. He doesn't come to school the next day. Or the next.

It isn't until Thursday that I start to worry.

Is he *dead*? Surely not, right? I didn't want to kill him or anything. Maybe just punish him a bit. Make him feel the way he makes me feel: like trash. Worthless for a while.

It's not until Friday that I finally see him. He sits with his head cupped in his hands when I enter the class. He doesn't bother to look up. His hateful eyes are obscured by a thick swoop of hair and his foot taps out an irregular beat on the floor. A frantic *tap! tap! tap!* that sends me to my desk a little faster. As I glide past him, he pushes a burst of air through his lips and a strange odor tickles my nose.

The sticky tack of glue fumes.

I watch Roger the entire class. There's something off about the way he sits, hunched forward like an arthritic eighty-year old. But there's something else. Something worse. His skin. It's taken on a strange chalky texture. Like drywall. Like it would crumble beneath my fingertips if touched. At one point, Roger feels the heat of my gaze and his eyes flick to mine. I quickly look away. For some reason, I expect him to know this was my fault. That I did this to him. But what I see staring back at me isn't anger.

It's fear.

A lake of it.

Cold. Clear. Fear.

It's crisp outside as I roll up to the curb and wait for Dad to pick me up. I shiver in my windbreaker and wonder how late he'll be today. Yesterday it was half-an-hour. The day before, forty-five minutes and reeking of booze. If he's that late today, I'll freeze.

A shrill whine snaps me out of the thought. An ambulance. Distant, but coming closer. Then I hear the cry. Roger's. Pain-drenched and terrified—like he's burning alive. He stumbles from the soccer field arms draped around two of his jock friends. Two cheerleaders swirl in front of them like gnats, screaming for help.

As they near, I squint and try to see what's wrong. His legs seem okay. His arms fine. Nothing's broken, but his face is all twisted up and his hands, they're . . . flapping. Like a pair of panicky birds. Dripping watery-pink fluid everywhere. And—*Oh, God*—the skin. . .

It's *gone*.

All of it.

In its place, fibrous red muscle entwined with nerve endings. Strips of bone peak through the tissue. And there's something else. Sticky white clumps of—*paste?*—speckled all over his palms. His forearms. It coats his naked digits and runs up to his wrists where the skin is peeling back in tattered strips.

I choke back a slug of bile.

The gym teacher, Mr. Johnson, abandons his post directing traffic and sprints over. "What happened?"

One of Roger's friends looks up wild-eyed, the spray of freckles over his nose suddenly dark in the afternoon sun. "It—it just—" He looks away and shakes his head, turns back, tears spilling through his lashes. "His skin just came off, Mr. Johnson. Like a pair of gloves. We were playing catch, and Roger started screaming when he caught the ball. We didn't know what happened at first..."

Roger unleashes a painful howl that cuts through my chest.

I did this to him. *I* made this happen.

A moment later, the ambulance tears up to the curb and I watch the EMTs load Roger up, his eyes wild with pain, rotating in their sockets like dirty, brown marbles.

That night, my eyelids scrape open to sheer darkness. A tomb. I can't see the streetlight through my blinds. Can't find the assuring glow of my alarm clock on my dresser. My torso is greased with sweat.

Roger's skin . . . I can't stop thinking about it. The way it sloughed off like boiled meat. The way it—

A chill washes over my arms, down my legs.

Someone's watching me.

I can *feel* it.

I can feel *him*.

My mouth goes sandpaper dry, my tongue swelling in my mouth. I can't handle him tonight. I can't give him another name and do this to someone else. Do what I did to Roger. I won't, I'll—

"N—Nick? Are you awake?"

Piper. My heart assaults my ribs. She can't come in here, not *now.*

Not with *him* watching.

But he's only ever talked to me, never to her. In more than a year. And there's something wrong with her, I can feel the panic radiating off her in waves. Can hear it in her voice.

She *needs* me.

"Hey, there, yeah. You okay?" I ask.

"Can I sleep with you tonight?"

"Don't be silly," I say, trying to mask the sudden tremor in my voice. "Of course, you can. Get in here." She used to sleep with me all the time when she was little, used to slip into my room clutching her teddy bear and complaining of nightmares. Really, it was when the fighting got too rough. Back when Dad would lose his temper with Mom and the snap of his voice would pour through the house like cold thunder.

But that was years ago, and now she's ten, sprouting knobby knees and braces, her features blooming into those of a young woman. Every time I look at her it hurts. That waterfall of brown-chocolate hair and the bubble nose. The warm olive skin that's so different than mine. All I see is Mom. Piper's all I have left of her.

I drape an arm around her as she slides beneath the sheets and I realize she's shivering.

"Hey, hey, what's the matter? You have a bad dream or something?"

She shakes her head and, her hair tickles my chin.

"What then?"

"It was—" She shudders, lets out a sob.

"Go on. You can tell me. You know that, right?"

She nods her head and lies quiet for a long moment before saying, "It was Dad. He was in my room again."

I stiffen, every wasted muscle in my body snapping taught. My throat glues shut as I run a hand over her head and soothe her until her breathing evens out. Then I lie wide awake, the blood hammering against my eardrums, like the day I found Mom in the bathroom with the empty bottle and the pills scattered around her fingers like snowflakes. Dead-eyed and foaming at the mouth, she lay there motionless and cold, the hem of her sweater hiked up just enough for me to see the purple patch of skin peeking through.

Dad always liked to keep his handiwork hidden.

I lie cardboard stiff and wait. And wait. And wait. For hours, staring at the wall, unable to sleep. Near three A.M., I finally catch a flicker of movement above my headrest. A serriform grin.

I say his name.

In the morning, I wake Piper and have her help me into my wheelchair. The kitchen has been fitted for me—the one thing Dad's done right around here—so I make a breakfast of scrambled eggs.

Sausage and orange juice and toast just like Mom used to on Saturday mornings, called them her *Weekend Specials*. There's nothing special about this morning, though. Piper sits there dead-eyed, head in hand, pushing the food around her plate until it's time for the bus.

When she stands to leave, I grab her arm.

"Hey, that stuff with Dad. It's never going to happen again. Ever. I promise. You don't have to worry about him anymore, okay?"

She remains frozen in place, her lips pressed into a thin line.

"Okay?"

Her delicate jaw bunches tight and she issues a quick nod, her eyes glassing over with tears, her gaze drifting to the floor.

She doesn't believe me.

But she should.

After she leaves, I wheel myself to Dad's door and burn my gaze into it. My fingers vice-grip the armrests of my wheelchair, clenching and unclenching and clenching again until my forearms feel like blocks of cement. Finally, after an hour, I knock once, twice.

I expect to hear his voice groggy and graveled over with sleep, expect for him to yell at me to go away like he does every morning when I wake him for my ride to school.

Nothing.

Hesitantly, I push it open and roll through. Dust motes clutter the air and the carpet is scattered with dirty laundry: greasy teeshirts and jeans and boxers. A crumpled construction vest. An empty bottle of Jack Daniels lies cockeyed on his dresser and the room reeks like he hasn't opened a window in weeks. The blinds are drawn and, as I roll through the gloom toward his bed, I catch sight of his crumpled form beneath the blankets.

"Dad?" I ask.

Silence.

I ask again.

More silence.

I reach out and clutch the comforter, hesitate; the last time I woke him after a night on the bottle I got a black eye for my trouble. I clench my jaw and give it a tug. Another one. The comforter rustles down over something thin and fibrous, inch-by-inch, until it appears.

Wallpaper.

Miles of it.

The ugly brown and yellow striped stuff on the walls of his room. It blossoms beneath his bed and runs up and over his arms, his torso, his legs. Encases his skull and stretches taught over the outline of his gaping mouth. I can't tell for certain, but his eyes appear to be stretched wide and his head is angled back in a sick fashion that makes me think he saw it coming.

I find a crease in the wallpaper near his chest and take hold of it.

Pull.

A sprinkle of sand shivers through.

I pull harder and a stream of it spills onto the bed and scatters to the floor. I know I should stop. That I should turn and wheel myself from the room, but I can't, my fingers working as if operated by a sick puppeteer. As I unwrap the Wallpaper Man's cancerous gift, beads of sweat erupt across my forehead, my back. And then I'm ripping it off in chunks, tearing it open like a toddler on Christmas anxious for his shiny new toy. Except what reveals itself is anything but shiny; rivulets of sand drift down to expose a pale cathedral of bone.

His ribcage.

Nausea churns through my intestines and I nearly retch, but somehow keep ripping, tearing the wallpaper off a pitted femur, a wrist bone.

His skull.

It's bleached-white and vacant, the eye sockets two black pits of tar peeking through the grit.

I slip the comforter back up and glide out of the room, drifts of sand crunching beneath my wheels, my stomach assaulting itself, spasming with disgust. But also, a sick satisfaction that it's finally over.

Piper never has to worry again.

Piper.

He's warned me.

The Wallpaper Man won't stop without a third name.

I know who he wants.

The thought sends a wave of gooseflesh rippling down my arms.

That *can't* happen, *won't* happen. I have his final name; I've had it all along.

But first I need to make a call.

I wait for hours, the house creaking around me as I sit in the silence of my room and stare at the wallpaper: toy bears marching with trumpets, leading a troupe of stuffed animals through a candy-

cane forest. Rabbits and deer and bug-eyed badgers following behind, each with an instrument of their own. A crazy, never-ending
parade. It's awful stuff—probably some baby's room before I moved
in. Likely a boy's room, based on the heavy bent toward blues and
yellows. Dad said he'd take the stuff down in a couple weeks.

Yeah right.

Decayed fragments of light peek in around the curtains, tell
me it's getting late. Aunt Lauren will be here soon. A half-an-hour or
so. She'll stop me if she gets here before I do this. I could barely hang
up on her as it was. One look at her, and all my strength will drain
into the floor.

I can't wait any longer.

From my lap, I take the steak knife and press it against the
left pad of my palm, feel its cold pressure dig into my skin.

Stop.

Moisture frames my vision. I don't *want* to do this. I don't
want to *die*. Even if I don't have that long left as it is. The thought of
never seeing Piper smile again, of never hearing her laugh or wave
at me from her bike. Never being able to tell her that I love her. That
everything will be okay.

Because it will.

Aunt Lauren loves Piper almost as much as I do. Like Mom
did. She'll take good care of her. Better than I could, anyways. And
she won't let her see this—what happened to Dad, what's about to
happen to me. She'll protect her. She'll give her the childhood she
deserves. The childhood I can't.

I've never seen the Wallpaper Man during the day. I don't
even know if this will work, but I have to try. I have to give him his
name, and I have to do it right now.

Before it's too late.

I bring the knife back into place, and a trickle of red bubbles
up around the blade. I hiss and grit my teeth so hard it feels as if my
molars will crack. I slide the blade the length of my lifeline and
nearly pass out.

The pain is exquisite.

Somehow, I manage to keep it together and roll myself over
to the wall. My blood looks black as oil as I press it against the wallpaper and hold it there.

I say my name.

Nothing happens.

I can feel the blood pulsing out of the wound in thick torrents, turning the wallpaper sticky—slick. My head goes woozy, and I struggle to focus. I whisper my name again.

Still nothing.

My hand slips an inch.

Two inches.

Catches.

Wallpaper coated fingers.

Around my wrist.

A sudden, piercing cold rips through my arm, mixing with the warm gush of blood on the wall.

"*I takes the pain, yes?*"

"Yes."

"*Yessshhhh.*" The hiss is otherworldly, eternal, reverberating through my chest and washing down my legs in awful, undulating torrents.

The fingers unfurl, and I thump back into my chair unable to move, unable to blink. I can only stare dumbly at my wrist, at the ring of crusted black skin flaking off where the fingers held me. I've never known pain like this before; it's like holding my hand in a sizzling pan of bacon grease.

A sheering sound brings my attention back to the wall where a single talon-coated finger at least ten inches long cuts through the vinyl material in a clean, vertical line. Then, through the rift, another digit emerges. And another and another. So many fingers spilling through that I lose count. At least a dozen in all, maybe more. Black, knotted knuckles. Cruel-looking blades extending from each fingertip. They are impossibly long and pop and croak as they curl in and out.

"*Don't be afraid. I takes the pain. I takes it all away.*"

A gust of something foul spills through the rift, a noxious rot that sours my nostrils and sets my eyes to watering. I blink away the tears and stare dumfounded at the hundreds of miniature patches of wallpaper tearing away from the wall and migrating toward the hand, crawling like maggots over one another and slithering onto its palm, leaving sticky trails of something mucous-like behind. Before my eyes, they writhe and contort and twist into one another in sick, disjointed motions, combining to sprout wings and antennae and hungry, sucking mouths. I watch in disgust, unable to avert my eyes from the seizing horde as it convulses into something I recognize.

Butterflies.

Dozens and dozens of wallpaper butterflies.

A burst of rot spills through once more, and before I can make a sound, they take flight and hurtle toward me with terrifying speed. Their razor-sharp wings lash against my skin, their stabbing legs piercing my flesh.

I gag and choke on their rotten bodies as they work down my throat and burrow into my stomach, into the soft gelatin of my eyeballs. Pure agony swims through every cell of my being as they shred through muscle and bone alike, my life spilling out of me in a thousand cuts at once.

Gray.
White.
Muted, colorless shades.
I am everything, everywhere, all at once.
Flicking into existence.
My new body feels strange, electric.
Dangerous.
A girl's room.
I can tell by the mountain of stuffed animals bulging from the corner hammock: Dogs and cats and smiling monkeys. A jewelry case frosts a white dresser. Posters of boy bands and horses coat the walls. Beaded necklaces are draped over a rocking chair, and in the corner, beneath a plush bedspread, a spray of hair drifts lushly over a pillow. It's hard to see the color through the striped wallpaper—it's dark—maybe amber, maybe brown—I can't quite tell with my new eyes.

All four of them.

Caleb Stephens is a CPA and author who resides in Denver, Colorado. His short stories have received honorable mentions in Writer's Digest 2016 Popular Fiction Awards and Allegory Magazine. His short story "Homecoming" will be published in a forthcoming 2018 Ink Stains Anthology by Dark Alley Press. His writing tips can be found on *The Writing Cooperative,* an online magazine focused on helping people write better. He is currently neck deep in his second novel, a dark psychological thriller that keeps him up way too late at night. When he's not writing, he can be found honing his guitar chops or playing with his three young daughters. Learn more about his work at www.calebstephensauthor.com and follow him on Twitter and Medium @cstephensauthor.

A DUEL AT DAWN
By Tom Lund

The place of the duel was a popular one for the purpose of felling prideful men, set just across the Hudson below the stone palisades that lifted Weehawken above New York. It was just after dawn as my men rowed across the river, and I stared past the oars that rowed like clockwork, pushing me ever closer my fate. But as I looked into the still dark water, I wondered at the depth of fear that must be running through my opponent, for I knew the reputation that preceded me.

That is not to say I have ever been a violent or bellicose man. In fact, for better or worse, I can say I have never been the one to issue a challenge. Our emerging politics have, in the years since the revolution, often required me to stand up to those seeking to elevate their own positions at the expense of our new country. I have a talent for pushing men to the edge of their honor—to that murky water where only pride navigates. But just as I've never issued challenge to another, I've also never stood down—and countless have fallen as a testament to such designs.

Many have speculated as to what my secret is, desperately searching for some way to explain how a man makes it through as many duels as I. They whisper the stories to one another in dark tavern corners, and yet I hear them. They tell stories of a curious flint that never fails to strike—a gift from an old war chief. Others say I sold my soul for an aim as true as the bible.

But they all have it wrong. There is no chance in this world, by their figure. There is only providence. Even the best marksmen, they say, could not guarantee such results—rightly so. And though there is indeed a secret to my survival, it lies not in a curious flint, nor in some deal with the devil.

Though I never would have articulated such, the explanation is simple: I was chosen. Long before the duels, long before the war, long before I was old enough to think about death, I was chosen for life.

I speak not of the Almighty above who dictates providence and watches over the earth, nor of His opposite, the great adversary. No, I mean something much darker than even the devil, and far older than such notions of Heaven and Hell.

I mean that ageless city, the myths of which we all remember, but never speak of. Dark and forgotten beneath the waves, its name would surely have caused Salem's witches to shudder, for even the most vile and wicked rituals of the black mass dared not invoke the name of Daws.

As sure as a glimpse of Daws meant certain death was approaching, a mere utterance of its name instilled an unfathomable anxiety that shook one to the very soul. Yet I saw it many times in my life with no consequence, and as such have felt free to invoke the dread city's name without fear, though few would ever have wished to hear it.

The first time I came upon Daws, I was but a child of ten hunting with my father in the steep Appalachian forest. I was farther out from our home than I was wont to wander and, at that point, quite turned around, but I moved with an urgency that only an angry father can instill. My father had gone off to the other side of the holler to push the deer from where they bedded down, leaving me to meet them farther downhill—though I knew not exactly where. I just kept forward, swift and silent in avoiding the cracking of dry and frosted leaves that gave alert to the beasts.

The sky was somehow a darker grey than the frozen oaks, and the clouds moved northerly in a chaotic grace that enthralled me. Whether I stared out of fear or fascination I knew not, but my father's teachings came to mind, and I knew only the severest of storms came from the north. Lost and shivering in the falling snow, I knew I needed to find my father.

But as I lowered my eyes from the wintry tempest dancing above, my gaze fell on something entirely out of place—a series of spires rising just over the ridge above me. They were strangely dark, and all my senses could scarce take in their immensity. The impossible structures dwarfed the surrounding mountains. I wondered how I could have never seen the immensity before.

Climbing the steep holler to have a closer look, I came to a grand stone wall that stretched as far as I could see in both directions, holding in its embrace an entire city. It was unearthly black from base to belfry, and every surface seemed to course like water running through drowned coals. I stood frozen there for some time, awestruck by the bizarre sight. But a winter fog soon moved in and hid the city from my view.

I knew not that I looked upon Daws until later when I awoke before the hearth of my home, my mother holding me in her arms. I still remember her tears and how they suddenly stopped when I recounted my tale of the mysterious black city.

She turned to my father. "Could it be?"

"You know the stories as well as I. Daws usually emerges in water—but not always."

My mother held me tighter at his words, and her terror screamed through her fingertips. She shook her head. "But what are we to do? No one lives after seeing Daws."

"Our boy did." He knelt with us in the warmth of the fire and put his hand on my shoulder. "You've seen the only place where Heaven and Hell have no dominion. I don't understand it, son, but where so many have peered through the black veil and met their doom, Daws chose you for life." He stared through both of us as he spoke, still grappling with all the tales of Daws he would soon come to share with me. Nodding his head ever so slightly, he said, "You were chosen."

And so I was chosen. It was a thought that I carried to every duel, and this morning was no different. A box sat at the center of the boat, and though all aboard knew what the box held, it was covered by a linen cloth so that all could swear they had not seen a weapon that morning. As regular a practice as this had become for me, it was nonetheless an unlawful contest frowned upon by much of high society, and I wished to save my men of as much culpability as possible in these circumstances.

Once on land I carried the pistols to the place of the contest, waiting for my opponent to call for my apology one last time. And as so many others in duels past, he would receive no such satisfaction. A man satiated wholly by apology has no business challenging another, even if compelled by honor. And only men who comprehend not their small place in this world live by such follies as honor.

That is not to disparage the man. Even before this morning I knew him to be neither a fool nor a coward. Just as I, he had thrown in his lot with the Continentals and fought long the whole war. I have even heard tell that he also was on York Island when the British landed at Kip's Bay.

I had served under Putnam, and my opponent under Washington, as we made preparations for potential landing. But our two regiments were separated by the British landing, leaving us cut off in the south. It was here, in yet another moment of near certain doom, that I once again saw Daws.

Hours after the landing, Putnam led most of the regiment north, hoping to evade the British on lesser known country roads. I was in the last column to abandon New York, by that time running into a British force just beyond the city as we followed a small road near the Hudson. In the ensuing skirmish I was downed by a bullet in the leg and, unable to stand again and fight, crawled through the mess of scrambling men to find cover in some brush on the riverbank.

In the dying light of dusk, I found an overturned boat wedged into the brush with me and forced my weary body under the protection of its hull. It was but a small vessel, one which, by the look of the oars lying underneath, some local must come to often to fish. As darkness fell upon the bank, the sounds of gunshots died off, and I knew the rest of the column had managed to slip by and follow the path inland. But that meant the British were on all sides of me and, knowing that I could not catch up with my men in my condition, I resolved to lay there until all light was gone from the sky.

I lay in that coffin a few hours more and, with every strange noise of the night threatening death, I questioned ever more my father's belief that I was chosen. Should a man chosen for life so often look death in the face?

When I was sufficiently convinced that my way was clear, I peered out from below the boat and saw the last glow of sunset dying on the horizon. Knowing I should push out before the moon rose, I turned the vessel upright upon the water and dragged my body over to rest inside. I ripped pieces of my shirt and wrapped my leg as best I knew, but the rising moon soon began the show itself, and before long I could see the blood. It looked black in the faint glow of night, fully soaking the makeshift bandage and dripping down to the bottom of the boat.

Knowing my men headed to Washington's camp at Harlem, I hoped to row upriver unnoticed, and though I started the rowing swift and strong, I soon found myself quite drained, drifting in and out of perilous slumber. With blood pooled below my feet, I knew I was losing ground as I drifted and shook myself with a fury that would let no dead man sleep.

But as I again took the oars in hand I noticed the black of my blood now oozing forth from the boat, poisoning the waters of the Hudson that then shone so clear in the light of the moon. I rowed to flee its grasp, as the depth of its darkness unnerved me more than any thought of death, but by then it surrounded me, and I knew there was no escape.

Resigning myself to whatever unearthly fate awaited me upon the dark waters, I said aloud, if just to myself, "But was I not chosen for life?"

And as the last sound flew from my lips I saw the beasts rise from the water to tower over my boat, the priests of Daws. Their robes were as black as the water below, and as they emerged I could discern not where the water ended and they began. Only their faces shone through the darkness, their long, angular tusks curving around even longer snouts.

They stared at me with eyes empty and hollow, and I could see in each the reflection of Daws rising behind me. Horror filled my veins where the black blood should have been, and the faint horns blowing from within the city of doom was the last thing I heard.

I awoke to the morning sun and sounds of shouting. The men at Harlem had found me floating near the riverbank, delirious from blood loss. They marveled and wondered how I managed to survive, and though they never would have believed it, I knew it was the promise of Daws that kept me alive.

Having survived two glimpses of Daws would give any man the courage of Samson, and in the years since then I had killed perhaps just as many of my own countrymen. I reflected on this as we turned away from one another with pistols in hand. I could hear my second's voice, counting the steps as I limped away from my opponent, ready as always to allow him the first shot before I took my own. Though this did relieve me of culpability, I did it not to avoid legal charge. I did it not for the thrill, nor for the principle. It was all for those precious moments, when flint struck, and powder ignited, and I could see Daws through the clouds of smoke.

From his childhood in the Caribbean to his later years in the Eastern Bloc, **Tom Lund** has found that sometimes the best way to explore this crazy world is to create your own.

It was the discovery of Lovecraft, Mirrlees, and Asimov in his late twenties that inspired Tom to start writing. With such a strange compass of inspiration driving his work, Tom hopes to navigate all horrific and fantastical realms of the speculative.

Tom resides with his wife and toddler son in the deserts of Southern Utah. In addition to his novels and short fiction, he also loves to tell stories through art and animation on Instagram.

Feel free to connect with Tom:
misterlugg@gmail.com
https://www.instagram.com/mrlugg/
http://www.mrlugg.com/

THE SKULL
By Drew Nicks

"What is it?"

"I don't know."

The two boys, Stinky and Jeff, stood staring down at the skull in the damp chill of the autumnal forest. Both boys had their jackets cinched up to their necks.

"I've never seen anything like that before," said Stinky.

"Me neither," replied Jeff.

Stinky picked up a stick that lay nearby. Making sure he was far enough away to bolt if necessary, he prodded the bleached white cranium. Jeff grimaced.

"What are you doing!" Jeff said. "What if it does something?"

Stinky laughed.

"Like what? It's clearly dead."

With a poke of the stick, the marble-like skull came free from its dirt grave. The more it shifted, the stranger its appearance became. It's shape and antlers reminded them of a caribou, though something about its proportions seemed wrong.

"Looks like one of the skulls Dad hung on the front of the house," Stinky said.

"Look at the teeth on it though."

The boys gazed along the elongated jaws of the mystery skull. The shimmering bone extended much too far to be a caribou. The teeth weren't right either. Instead of the normal square shape, the skull possessed long, pointed, daggers. The entire tableau gave the boys the heebie-jeebies. A loon called out somewhere in the distance.

"This thing gives me the creeps," said Jeff. "Let's go home."

Stinky shot his brother a smirk. His glance gave Jeff a chill.

"You're not scared, are ya?"

Jeff, with true boyhood naiveté, cracked a smile at his brother. *It's just a stupid skull!*

"I'm not scared of nothing."

He bravely walked over to the shape, and, to prove his brother wrong, placed his hand upon it.

It was warm and dry. It shouldn't be, but it was. Jeff looked into the inky sockets. Though whatever it had been was devoid of life, he swore he could feel a shudder in the dry bones. He quickly pulled his hand away. Stinky started to laugh.

"Jeff is a fraidy cat! Jeff's a fraidy cat!"

Jeff broke from the weird feeling that had been coursing through his body and rushed his brother. He pushed him to the damp ground. Stinky laughed the entire way.

"Shut up!" Jeff hollered. "I am not a fraidy cat! You are!"

Stinky stood up and brushed the wet dirt from his jacket. He scowled.

"Well, if you're not scared, let's bring it home for Dad to see. Dad'll know what it is. Dad knows everything."

The thought of bringing the strange thing home with them excited Jeff. Though the skull gave him an uneasy feeling, he knew that Dad could ease that feeling. Stinky was right, Dad did know everything.

With assurance now in their sights, the boys each grabbed an antler and lifted the skull with all their might. To their surprise, it weighed next to nothing. The brothers smiled as they carried their prize back into town

Stony Rapids had never been a big community. It only received its first post office twenty-five years prior. Not much tourism either, outside of the occasional whitewater rafter and "survivalist." Most of the community got a good laugh at the "survivalists." Those who had lasted more than one winter knew what it meant to survive. The city-folk were jokes. None would say it out loud in their presence, though. No one wanted to jeopardize that extra cash.

The Tomlinson house was on the edge of Stony Rapids. The back porch opened up directly onto the majestic pine forest. Archie Tomlinson was chopping wood for the upcoming winter when he saw his boys emerge from the tree line. His powerful arms split the last piece of pine, and he watched the object they carried between them. He set the axe down and called out to them:

"Hey boys, what have you got there?"

The brothers rushed over to their father, excitement plastered across their faces. Dad was still focused on the skull they had.

"Dad!" they called in unison.

When they reached him, they put the skull on the ground at his feet.

"Look what we found!" Jeff said.

"You mean, what I found," Stinky added snidely.

Jeff pushed him and was pushed back. Jeff threw Stinky to the ground and climbed on top of him with a small fist in the air. Dad lifted Jeff off his brother with one hand.

"I don't care who found it," Dad scolded. "I just want to know what you boys found."

All three stared down at the skull at Dad's feet. A sudden, chill breeze swept over them. The two boys shivered while Dad seemed unfazed. He had felt much worse.

Dad knelt and looked at it. It wasn't a caribou. He immediately noticed the sharp teeth and enormous jaws. *What the fuck?* He lifted it up and looked closely. Now that he was eye level with it, there seemed to be so much wrong with it. The eye sockets weren't where they should be. They were located where a human's eyes would sit. Something about the nose was strange too. This he couldn't quite pinpoint. Perhaps it was the nostrils. Perhaps it was its stoutness. Something just seemed off.

"Where did you boys find this?"

The boys looked to each other. Neither was sure what to say. They could tell that the skull had a strange effect on their father. After a moment, Stinky finally spoke up:

"We found it out in the woods. It was kind of covered in dirt."

Dad put the skull down and looked out into the tree line. The branches and pine needles fluttered in the chill breeze. A loon called mournfully from the nearby Fond du Lac River. A stern look crossed Dad's face.

"Go on into the house boys. Tell your mother that I'll be back in a little bit."

Both boys looked up at their father; expressions of incredulity across their faces. But, knowing their father, they knew it unwise to disobey him. They quickly ran up the three steps, past the mounted caribou skulls and rickety rocking chair, and into the house. Before they went to their mother, they crept up to the living room window and watched Dad. In the yard, Dad picked up the skull and hauled it off out of sight. The brothers assumed that he had taken it to the woodshed. When he returned to sight, he walked to the chopping block. He leaned down and lifted the axe up. For a few moments, he stood there, his eyes scanning the woods. They could see their father take a deep breath, mutter something beneath his breath, and set off towards the sky-reaching pines.

Several hours later, with the boys huddled close to the fireplace, their mother glancing to the front door every few moments, Dad came home. The boys were shocked from their positions by the sudden opening of the door. Dad flew in with such force that an old bear trap above the fireplace fell and hit the wood floor. It snapped shut.

The first thing that the boys noticed about Dad was the pallid tone of his skin, his sweat-streaked face. He turned rapidly and slammed the door shut, hoisted the bar for the door and threw it home. When he turned again to face his family, the boys noticed something else smeared on his clothes.

Blood.

"Get the boys upstairs, Hannah!" Dad yelled.

Mom stood there for a moment, fear across her face.

"Now! Before it gets in!"

As if on cue, the front door began to rattle in its hinges. Stinky and Jeff looked wide eyed at one another. In an instant, Mom had swept the two into her arms with unnatural speed and ran upstairs with them. She stopped in front of their shared room and let them down. The banging against the front door was nearly deafening, but, intermittently, the boys could hear their father screaming at the unseen intruder.

"What's going on, Momma?" Stinky asked. "Why was Dad covered in blood?"

Mom looked her boys over. They had never seen their mother with such sad and confused eyes before.

"I don't know, Stinky. I just don't know."

Jeff carefully watched his mother. There was something about her tone that wasn't right. It seemed to him that she was leaving something out.

"But, Momma..."

Just then, a new flurry of fury slammed into the front door. They could hear Dad hollering at the intruder in some strange language. Then, they heard Dad loading the shotgun. Mom looked at her boys tearfully.

"Just go into your room, boys. Everything will be all right soon. I'll come and get you."

And, like that, Mom had disappeared downstairs. They could hear her join in Dad's attempts to blockade the door. The boys thought about spying on the situation but then thought better of themselves. They sped into their room. Stinky sat on his bed waiting, while Jeff hid himself beneath his blankets.

After a time, the chaos calmed. The boys could no longer hear the intruder trying to force entry, though both of them refused to move from their positions. They thought to themselves that if it was enough to scare Dad, they didn't want to see it. So they sat and waited. Through the creaky floorboards, they heard snippets of conversation. Mom and Dad seemed very heated. Dad sounded exhausted.

"... I don't know, I went out into the woods after the boys brought that skull back," said Dad. "Then, I don't know. I think it's come back..."

Mom's comments were muffled. Though the boys leaned close to the floor, they couldn't make out her words. Dad's voice took over again:

"I know, Hannah. I thought it was done too. I don't even know how they found it. The woods are like a maze sometimes..."

Dad mumbled a few more words. For a while, silence pervaded their parents. Then they heard Mom stand and head towards the kitchen. They heard Dad's eerie statement he had intended for their Mom.

"Watch out for the neighbors, Hannah. Winter comes early this year..."

The next morning, the snow began to fall. The boys excitedly ran out front and started making snowballs. Meanwhile, Mom and Dad stood on the porch with concern running between them. Dad put his arm around Mom and drew her close. He kissed her on the forehead and they watched their boys enjoy the little bit of winter they could. They enjoyed the serenity. They laughed when they saw Jeff throw one before Stinky could retaliate. Dad held Mom and they felt like a proper family, until they saw Fred Pratt walking up the driveway. He walked with a certain stumble. A stumble Dad had seen many times before.

"What did you do, Tomlinson?" called Fred Pratt. "What fresh hell have you dumped upon us?"

The boys, who had been preoccupied with their tomfoolery, saw the emaciated Pratt. His appearance frightened them so much that they ran to the porch and hid behind their parents. Fred Pratt did not halt his advance.

"What have you done to the town, Tomlinson? There is no appeasing him now. You have brought death and degradation to everyone!"

Stinky grabbed Dad's hand. Jeff hid behind Mom and whimpered.

"Dad?" inquired Stinky. "What's he talking about? He's scaring me."

Dad looked down at his eldest boy and offered him a reassuring smile. He looked to Mom and nodded, indicating it was time to bring the boys inside. She drew her arms around the boys and led them in, while they heard Dad uncovering the shotgun on the porch. They could still hear the mumbled yet frantic words of Fred Pratt.

From the warm confines of the house, they could hear Dad arguing with Pratt. They could only make out some of the argument. Mom kept trying to shoo them from the door, though she knew it was pointless:

"Get off my property, Fred! You don't need to come around here and scare my boys like that."

"Do you even know what you've done, Tomlinson? Don't you remember? I've got a wife and kids of my own. My youngest went missing last night. . ."

"I don't have anything to do with that, Fred. You'd best get on home."

"Don't tell me what to do, you sick bastard! Are you going to bring little Richie back? Or did you take him? Did you give him to that thing?"

The boys heard Dad cock his shotgun. For a few seconds, all beyond the door was silent. They knew this would not last long.

"Don't make me tell you again, Fred. Get off my property or things are going to get much worse."

They heard Dad step off the porch. They heard the gravel kicked up by his boots. Fred Pratt sounded like he was about to add something when the shot rang out.

"I told you to get off my property, Pratt! Now go on, get!"

The boys heard the sudden kick of stones in the yard. They reckoned that Fred Pratt had taken off running. Then they listened closely to his final words:

"I'll go, Tomlinson, but when it comes, don't expect me to help. You and your family are dead to me. . ."

A minute later, Dad walked in the front door. His face was pale, and his eyes were bloodshot. He kept licking his lips. The boys looked with wide pupils up to their looming father. He still carried the shotgun in his hands. Carefully, he set it down against the wall and, without a word, walked to the sofa. He slumped down on it, shut his eyes and quickly drifted off to sleep. The boys stared at Dad. They had never seen him fall asleep so fast.

"Boys! What are you doing?" said Mom; they hadn't noticed her silent figure in the kitchen doorway. "Let him sleep."

The boys did as they were told. They walked over towards Mom. She knelt to look them in the eyes. Gazing at the children she created, she smiled.

"Why don't you boys help me in the kitchen? Lunch is almost ready."

The boys, their cares soon forgotten, eagerly ran off into the kitchen. They elbowed each other trying to get to the refrigerator first. Mom smiled. She knew that this display of emotion was an empty one. While Dad slept soundly on the sofa, she made her way to the door and nudged the bar into place. *May god pity us*, she thought.

The sky was lit with a strange green hue and the wind whipped heavily against the house, blowing snow over the frost covered windows. The inhabitants of the house could hear the scream of the wind through the cracks in the walls and around the windows. Stinky and Jeff could not sleep. They sat in their room on their beds exchanging glances and grimaces. Stinky, though he didn't like to admit it, was terrified of the dark. Jeff always knew this but never gave his brother a hard time about it. He didn't see any point. Stinky never exposed Jeff's fears and Jeff appreciated that. They were two peas in an all concealing pod.

That night, Stinky was terrified of the light. The green of the sky turned his stomach in knots and his eyes welled tears along their edges. They sat there and watched the shades of color dance along the walls, when they heard a blood curdling scream overtop the harsh wind. At first, the boys thought it came from within the house. They bolted down the stairs only to find Mom and Dad standing quietly and watching the front door. When they came close, they saw that Dad was eyeing the bar.

"Daddy. . ." Stinky said weakly.

Stinky never called him Daddy. Jeff looked over to his older brother and saw him shaking violently. A trickle of urine dribbled down his pajama leg. Despite the smell of ammonia filling the room, Dad grabbed Stinky and held him close.

"It's okay, Stinky. Everything is going to be okay."

Just then, another scream cut through the whipping night air. Jeff grabbed tightly onto Mom's hand. She squeezed back. Dad shivered noticeably, and a sweat began to build along his face and forearms. *Something's coming.*

"Go on to bed, boys," said Dad.

"But, Dad," said Stinky. "I can't sleep. The light makes my tummy hurt. . ."

Dad suddenly swiveled and looked down sharply at his son. He knelt with a severe look in his eyes.

"Go to bed, Stinky. Go to bed NOW!"

Stinky looked up at Dad and shook violently. His eyes trembled. Little wrinkles formed in his little forehead. He burst into tears and fell to the floor, wallowing in his own urine. Dad snapped. He picked Stinky up and slapped him hard across the face. Stinky stopped crying.

"Go to bed, boys. NOW! DO YOU UNDERSTAND ME?"

Both boys, terrified, ran up the stairs and into their room. Stinky let the tears flow and embraced his brother. Jeff, despite the odor, held Stinky tight. From out in the night, the woodshed pulsated. An ethereal glow blazed out on the encroaching woods.

Both boys lay in their beds that night but neither slept.

The next morning, the sun did not rise. Stinky and Jeff were too terrified to leave their room, though they heard the murmurs of conversation coming from the floor below. Unlike before, they couldn't hear any of what was being said. They soon felt the chill of the winter blowing in from the open front door, then they heard it slam shut. Footsteps resonated through the house as they heard Mom climbing the stairs. The door opened a crack and lamplight crept in. Both boys stared at the door. When she saw that both boys were wide awake she entered. Her cheeks were moist. She sat down on Jeff's bed.

"What's wrong, Momma?" Jeff asked.

She was about to speak when something stopped her. She brought a hand to her face to halt the tears that were forming anew. Jeff got out from under the covers and crawled over to Mom. He took her other hand in his. She gripped it tightly.

"Your father went over to the Pratt's house. He wanted to check on them. He said he . . . he. . ."

She couldn't hold back any longer and she collapsed on the small bed. She cried until the blanket beneath her became damp. Stinky and Jeff looked at each other with deep concern across their faces. They had never seen Mom like this. Mom was always a strong-willed woman and she knew that Dad could take care of himself. Then they thought about the screams last night and the sudden change in Dad's behavior. They left their nearly catatonic mother and crept downstairs.

The living room was deathly cold. It seemed to them that the front door must have been open for some time. The fireplace was black. No smoke or sparks emanated from the carbonized wood. Jeff stepped close to the front door and noticed items missing. Gone from the brackets where it normally hung, was Dad's shotgun. Also missing from the small table just inside the door, was his trusted Bowie knife. Mom had not reset the bar and the door was not fully closed. The wind made an awful wail through the slim opening. Jeff pushed the heavy door shut with some effort and tried to lift the bar. He was not strong enough.

"Stinky, come help me with this," he called to his brother.

Stinky stood close to the fireplace. He was mesmerized by the darkness outside and the snow blasting against the windows. Jeff snapped his fingers a few times in his sibling's direction. That broke the spell on Stinky and he joined his brother in replacing the bar. When they had it in place, they heard footsteps behind them.

"What are you doing, boys?"

They turned to look at their mother on the stairs. Her long brown hair hung over her face so that they could not see her mood.

She moved with awkward and stilted motions. Her legs lifted like that of a silent film actor. Her expressions seemed over exaggerated. The boys didn't know what to think.

"We were putting the bar back," said Jeff. "It's what Dad would've wanted."

She looked down at them and her head cocked at a strange angle, as though she were listening but not really conscious.

"That's good, boys," she said. "That's good. That's what Dad would've wanted. . ."

She trailed off like a stuck record. Robotically, she wandered over to the sofa and sat down. Her glazed eyes stared at the blackened fireplace. Stinky climbed up, sat next to her and joined in staring at the dead wood. Jeff thought that maybe they should get it started again. He could see his breath.

"Momma, should we start the fire again? I'm freezing. . ."

Mom turned her head deliberately. She stared at Jeff with cold, dead eyes. He could see the pronounced wrinkles along her cheeks.

"Yes Jeff, we should get the fire started again. I am freezing. . ."

Though she said it, she made no move to relight it. She would alternate between staring at the dead fireplace and the barred door. Jeff knew that Mom was helpless. Her mind could not focus. He walked over to the fireplace, took out the matches that Dad left upon the mantle and tried to light the carbonized wood. It wouldn't take. He tried again and still it would not take. Trying a third time, the match flared out beneath the frosty flue. Jeff's eyes began to fill with tears as desperation overtook him. Finally, a moment of lucidity overtook their mother.

"Jeff, honey, that won't light. Let Momma do it."

In one swift motion she was on her feet and loading chopped logs into the fireplace. She placed some newspaper beneath the wooden formation and lit the brittle, yellowed paper. The flames took; the room would soon be warmed by nature's incandescence. She looked over to Jeff who stood bawling. Streams of snot ran down his face. She walked over to him, drew him in close and led him to the couch. There they sat, beneath a warm blanket, awaiting Dad's return.

A twisting of the doorknob awakened Stinky and Jeff on the couch. Neither could be sure how long they had slept. The twisting of the knob continued. They looked to the window that flanked the door. They saw Dad. Or at least what looked like Dad. His face was red and feverish. The red was from the blood of the strange skins he wore along his head. The pinkish flesh continued to bleed along the contours of his face. His eyes were wide and maniacal. He groped along the fragile, frost covered glass. The knob continued to twist. Dad began to lick the windowpane. He smiled.

Mom woke up and spotted him. Automatically, she stood and walked towards the door. Jeff, in a panic, bolted upright and tried to stop her. At first she smiled down at him. Although he tried to pull her back, his little body could not hold her. He held on to her arm with all the dead weight he could manage. She paid little heed and kept moving forward. When Jeff tried to call to his brother, she whipped him from her arm, directly into the wooden wall. Dad smiled from his position in the window with eyes beckoning to his wife. She kept moving. She was at the door now. The knob continued to twist. Jeff knew there was no way that Dad was twisting that knob. He tried again to stop Mom, but she already had the bar off. The brutal winter chill swept into the house. . .

Drew Nicks has always been fascinated by horror. Continued viewings of *Jaws* and *Aliens* as a youth skewed his young mind. His work has been featured in Dark Corner Books, Road Maps and Life Rafts, and The Lovecraft Lunatic Asylum. He resides in Moose Jaw, Saskatchewan.

DREAMS OF THE WEREHOUSE
By Joshua Chaplinsky

Pete Gilman came to in an abandoned lot, vomit all down the front of him. *Not again*, he thought, as consciousness triggered a dance beat deep within his skull. He peeled his tongue from the roof of his mouth and tried to sit up. Every muscle in his body begged him not to. When he finally did, he noticed he'd lost one of his shoes. His clothes looked as though they'd gone on a bender of their own.

He walked until factories gave way to cheap housing and then finally familiarity. What had he been doing all the way out in Northwest Industrial? He didn't remember leaving the house last night. There was only a vague recollection of sweaty bodies, writhing together in the dark. —*writhing in pain/screaming not dancing*— He shook his head and the image dissipated. That explained the dance beat, at least. Considering where he woke up, they must have raised that party to the ground.

He shielded his eyes and looked up at the sky, experiencing a rare moment of appreciation for Portland's gloomy weather. He'd probably missed his shift at the storage facility, so he figured he might as well go home and take a nap.

He hit the pillow and slept like the dead, black and dreamless. When he woke for the second time that day it was to the sound of angry vacuuming. He stumbled out of his room to confront his mother, but thought better of it once he saw her face. He put on a pot of coffee and sat at the kitchen table. Pulled out his phone and texted Frank.

"Your boss called."

He looked up to meet his mother's penetrating gaze. He hadn't noticed she'd turned the vacuum off.

"What did he want?"

Mrs. Gilman shrugged her shoulders.

"I didn't ask."

She unplugged the vacuum and started wrangling the cord. Pete willed the coffee to brew faster.

"You know keepin' that job's a condition of your parole."

"I know, ma."

"And would it kill you to visit my grandson once in a while?"

My grandson. Never *your* son. If she cared so much, why didn't she support the kid?

The mere mention of his bastard child triggered the usual unpleasant reverie, wherein Pete tried to pinpoint exactly how he fucked things up so badly. Long story short, he'd met Lucy in rehab (the first time, before he violated parole and the judge sentenced him to six months) and didn't even remember consummating what many considered "The World's Shortest Relationship." But the paternity test took her side, so congratulations to him! He would have tried to talk her into an abortion, but he didn't find out about the pregnancy until after he got out of jail, and by that point there was no going back.

Pete retreated to his room, sans coffee. It didn't take long for Frank to arrive. They'd lived across the street from one another since grade school and neither had bothered to leave the nest. Yet Frank had somehow managed to achieve slackerdom without running afoul of the law.

Frank waited his turn as Pete took a long pull on the glass pipe and held it. For a brief moment, the chaos in Pete's brain crystallized. —*life is a collapsing building no one can escape.*— He coughed and sputtered, releasing a cloud of smoke into the room. The moment had passed. Frank laughed and extended greedy hands.

"We definitely didn't hang out last night?" Pete asked as Frank took his turn. Frank held his breath and shook his head.

"You told me you had to get up early for work." Thick smoke escaped with the words.

"Hm. . ." Pete turned his thoughts inward as the weed crept up on him. It put its hand on his shoulder, but when he turned around there was no one there. He'd never lost an entire night before.

"That good, huh?" Frank held the pipe out to him, a vicarious grin on his face. Pete waved him away.

"I need to get some food."

The duo munched away at their post-session burritos in silence. Pete could feel the meat between his teeth. —*like flesh/slowly rotting.*— It turned mealy in his mouth. He dropped the burrito on his tray.

"Thought you were hungry?" Frank said through a mouthful, a glob of refried beans smeared on his lips. Pete stared at his friend, overwhelmed with disgust. His stomach lurched. He had to steady himself with a hand against the table.

"So did I."

"Well, if you're not gonna eat it. . ." Frank moved the tray over to his side of the table. He alternated between the two burritos, bite for bite, picking up speed as he did. Frank ate fast when anxious, a nervous tick Pete would have recognized had he been paying attention.

"Listen," Frank said through the meat and cheese. "There's something I've been meaning to—"

Pete jumped up and sprinted for the restroom. Frank watched him go, open mouth displaying a mass of food. Once Pete disappeared around the corner, Frank resumed chewing at a normal pace, relieved the moment had passed.

Pete entered the bathroom and pressed his head against the cool porcelain of the urinal. He usually bounced back much quicker than this. Some sleep and a couple hits and he was right as the Stumptown rain. What had happened last night? He kept getting fleeting images. A smoky room with funhouse angles. Bizarre diagrams. Peals of laughter—or were they agonized screams? As soon as he focused on an image it dissipated. Maybe it was time to take his sobriety more seriously.

"You all right?"

Pete lifted his head. Saw a distorted Frank reflected in the urinal pipe, like one of the faces trapped in his memory.

"Come on," the reflection said, still chewing. "They're closing up."

Frank put an arm around Pete and helped him out of the restroom. Every time Pete blinked it acted like a jump cut in a movie.

Bathroom, *blink,* storefront, *blink,* sidewalk. Pete blinked his way across the parking lot when a girl's voice called out.

"Hey, I know you."

Even though he didn't recognize her, Pete could tell she was talking to him. He panicked internally as he tried to put a name to the face. Or a time or place.

"Surprised to see you up and running," the girl said. She had short black hair that matched her leather jacket and eyes that bordered on the same. Eyes devoid of an iris. "That was some party."

"Yeah." Pete tried to put as much confidence into the word as he could. It was the only word he had.

"Kez," the girl said. He didn't recognize the name, but something about the way she said it made the receptors in his brain itch.

"Right. Kez. Sorry."

The girl pulled out a pen and wrote seven numbers on the back of a burrito receipt. She held it out to him, made him walk over to get it.

"Let's do it again some time."

When their hands touched he got a quick flash of her sticking out her tongue, a paper square emblazoned with a cartoon rat centered in the pink of it. A rat with a man's face. She gave a mischievous smirk as she transferred the tab from her tongue to his with a kiss.

The memory faded to reveal Kez behind the wheel of her rusted-out '68 Cadillac Sedan. She flashed an identical smirk as she backed out of her parking spot and pulled away.

"There's that mystery solved," said Frank.

Kez called Pete the next day. Or had he called her? He didn't remember giving her his phone number. All he knew was he put his ear to the phone and heard her voice telling him when and where. All he said was yes.

She picked him up at his place. The next thing he knew they were sharing rat tabs in the Caddie out at Macleay Park, the moon glancing off the cracks in the windshield. They talked the usual drug talk—the existence of g/God(s), alternate dimensions—and then she was pressing her body against his.

"I want to be inside you," she breathed. —*a red door swings open/featureless faces push from within flesh-colored walls/screaming to get out*—Pete ignored the thought, and what was surely some sort of heat-of-the-moment grammatical malaprop. The chemicals in the rat tab were doing strange things to his head. In his paranoia he imagined vagrants surrounding the car, pressing against the fogged windows, watching them. What would stop them from opening the doors and settling into the backseat for a better view? What would stop Kez from offering them popcorn or devouring their souls? He pushed the image down, deep down, buried it inside himself as he unbuckled his pants.

—blood thrums/propelling ever forward/the moon eclipses the sun/flies buzz around its corona/attempt to pierce the membrane of light/a solitary insect succeeds/injects its saliva/follows the enzymes through the barrier/unravels into a million lines of code/the sun belching radiation/dividing and subdividing within itself/exploding in a white-hot ball of light—

Pete came to in a meadow, insects shrieking all around him. He put a hand to his head and rubbed his temple. *—your body is a temple/an altar made of flesh—* His double vision coalesced into a single image: a wall of weeds squared around him, his body at the center. Within the square and beneath him, the vegetation had been flattened as if by a large object.

The same weight seemed to press down on him as he tried to stand and failed, his muscles refusing to comply. Once again, his clothes were trashed. Luckily his phone hadn't died, and he still had a couple bucks, so he called for a cab. By the time he dragged himself to the edge of the park it had arrived.

The tiny TV in the back of the cab barked at him as they pulled away. Pete jabbed an angry finger at the speaker symbol to silence it. Leaned back and closed his eyes.

"You wanna be careful where you camp out," the driver said. Pete opened one eye. He poked his finger in the man's direction, wishing he could silence *him.* "Another homeless kid went missing last night."

—vagrant/wanderer/proxy/acolyte—

"I'm not fucking homeless." Pete closed his eye, but not before it caught the face on the screen, the girl the driver must be referring to. The second of two transients to vanish in as many nights. She didn't look familiar, with her disheveled pixie cut and soft bruises, but from behind a foggy window or screaming through a veil of flesh, maybe. . .

He put it out of his head. How can you even tell when a homeless person goes missing? Portland was where homeless people went missing *to*.

"Maybe you were, you know. . ." Frank pressed his lips together and made a noise like a hovering spaceship. This despite the fact he hadn't smoked up yet. "Lemme check for abduction marks." He reached over and pulled on the neck of Pete's shirt.

Pete pushed him away, got up from the bed and inspected his neck in the mirror. A cluster of pink bruises stood out against his pale skin.

"I think those are hickeys." He flopped back down on the bed. Frank shifted gears.

"Nice. You gonna see her again?"

"Tonight."

"Cool, cool. . ." Frank looked down at sweaty hands. They seemed to surprise him. "So, does that mean you and Lucy. . ."

Pete scowled.

"I'm sorry, I shouldn't have—"

A pillow to the face cut Frank off.

"It's bad enough I get that shit from my mother, I don't need to hear it from you too."

The next night Kez showed up at Pete's house with a friend. A girl with greasy blonde hair and dark bags under her eyes. She looked like Kez had picked her up off the street. Your typical Portland indigent.

"I hope you don't mind," Kez said, and the next thing he knew the friend had him pinned in the backseat of the Caddie while Kez drove aimlessly around town. At a certain point they stopped for cigarettes and the women switched places. After a succession of stops and switches, Pete lost track of which woman was which. And that was before the rat tabs.

They cruised through the streets of Northwest Industrial as time tied itself in knots. Their hungry pupils opened wide to devour the little light available. They yelled out the windows at the denizens of the night, both real and imaginary, inviting them to join the party. Eventually they convinced one such apparition to get into the car.

The guy grabbed his backpack and jumped into the backseat. He looked as if he hadn't been on the street long, but his eyes said otherwise. Pete had never experimented with guys before, but found himself going with the flow. If he closed his eyes he couldn't tell much of a difference.

From there reality became even more slippery. What little Pete retained cast him in the role of observer, not participant. He felt like a bystander at an orgy. His mind's eye everywhere at once. Those he watched seemed oblivious to him, and although he wasn't involved in the debauchery his body felt inhabited by those around him.

Each time they went out they found new people to play with. Some nights there was barely any room in Kez's boat of a car. They'd ride through the darkness, eventually winding up at some industrial space or abandoned art gallery. Reality and memory would diverge, shift out of sync. Each morning Pete woke up in a field or abandoned lot, amidst a pile of rubble or a square of flattened ground. Each morning he felt a little less like himself, a little more like a sum of the souls within his sphere. He lost track of the days he slept through as the nights bled into each other.

Pete drifted through the front door desperate for sleep, only to be confronted by Frank holding his infant son. Mrs. Gilman and Lucy looked on with approval as Frank shifted the child's weight like a bag of groceries. They painted a surreal portrait of 50s America. Norman Rockwell turned on in his ear.

"What's going on here?"

Frank practically dropped the baby. Luckily, Lucy scooped him right up. Mrs. Gilman's elusive smile disappeared, back from whence it came.

"That's what we're here to find out," she said, emphasizing the seriousness of the situation with a finger point. "You scared poor Lucy half to death last night."

Pete looked to the mother of his unwanted child.

"What the hell is she talking about, Lou?"

Lucy's eyes flitted back and forth between Pete and Mrs. Gilman. Mrs. Gilman continued.

"You don't remember, do you?"

"Obviously not." Pete scratched at his scalp, scattering a flurry of dandruff. He looked longingly towards his bedroom door.

"Probably because you were wacked out of your mind. What were you thinking, showing up at Lucy's with a car full of degenerates like that?"

A wave of déjà vu hit Pete. Some of what his mother said rang true. He saw himself stumbling across the lawn, Lucy on the porch. He held up a condescending finger.

"Correction. I showed up at Lucy's *parents'* house." He turned to Frank. "We're not the only ones who still live at home, you know."

His mother cut him off. "The point is, you're out of control."

"Calm down. I probably just wanted Lucy to come out and have some fun. You're always telling me I should spend more time with her."

His mother squinted fire at him. At least he'd shut her up. But then, another voice rose to the occasion.

"You weren't there for her."

The voice had come from Frank.

Pete turned to his friend. His friend, who only moments ago had been holding *his* son. Just like he'd been doing the night before, next to Lucy on her parents' porch.

"I see what's going on here." He turned his gaze on Lucy. It was all coming back to him.

"That's not what this is about," Frank said, empty hands twitching.

"It's not? Seems to me I wanted to spend some quality time with my son, but he had prior engagements."

"You threatened to kidnap him."

"Bullshit. You can't kidnap your own son."

"You said you wanted to feed him to the house."

The conversation came to a screeching halt, amplifying the silence that followed. Lucy pressed the child tight against her chest. —*the walls pulse with the rise and fall of breath/a child's cry echoes through the halls*—

Frank locked eyes on Pete.

"Do you know how crazy that sounds? Something about a one-for-one trade, for his shadow brother."

Pete looked away.

"That's not all." Frank pointed to a copy of the *Tribune* on the kitchen table. It featured half a dozen headshots crowned by the headline: MISSING TALLEY RISES. "Any of those look familiar?"

Despite the sunken, pockmarked skin, Pete recognized her immediately. The short black hair. The leather jacket. She had been the first one to disappear. Kez.

This is your face on drugs, Pete thought.

Next to her were other members of his party crew that had been reported missing. The most recent addition being Charlie Seether, an old high school buddy who had been in and out of rehab and bouncing around on couches for the better part of the last five years.

—Kez sinks her fingers into Charlie's chest, like a moist piece of cake—

"Impossible. I hung out with Kez last night."

—She licks the inside of him off her fingers as he screams—

"Maybe that's something you'd like to tell the cops."

Frank locked eyes with Pete yet again. Since when had he gotten so assertive? It threw off the equilibrium of their relationship. Pete panicked, pushed past his friend to take refuge in the safety of his room. But before closing the door, he turned back to his would-be interveners.

"You want to go to the cops? Be my guest. Tell them your crazy theory. But I don't have time for this bullshit."

He slammed the door. Toby's cry cut the silence.

"And get that kid out of here!" Pete yelled through the door.

Pete laid on top of the covers, fully dressed, listening to Lucy sniffle as she packed up the baby and left. It sounded like Frank went with her. That was an interesting development, one he should be happy about, but the thought only made him angry. Toby was *his* son. If he wanted to feed him to the house, that was his right.

—one for one/bring us your son—

Pete shook his head. Frank's paranoid nonsense was getting to him and he needed some sleep. He looked to the pipe on his bed stand but didn't reach for it. He needed a clear head, to think. He needed to dream, and not in a hypnagogic state. Kez was bad news. He knew that. His relationship with her wasn't a healthy one. He was either going to wind up back in jail or dead. And that shit with the missing persons . . . he had no idea what to make of that. All those people were alive and well and partying with him every night.

It felt like he'd only just closed his eyes when Kez roused him with two long honks. He'd told her he'd be outside waiting—he didn't want to alert his mother to his comings and goings, in case she planned on narcing on him—but he'd overslept. If the cops were lying in wait, they were about to hit the jackpot.

Pete grabbed his jacket and rushed out of the house, bouncing off Frank's chest not two steps from the door.

"What the hell, man?"

"I'm coming with you."

Pete surveyed the front yard. No cops. Only Frank.

"Were you hiding in my bushes?"

"I said I'm coming with you."

Pete looked over to the Cadillac idling in front of his house.

"It's okay," Kez called over. "We've got room."

Kez had been busy. They only had room for one more. —*one for one*—Pete sized up his friend. Concern belied his anger.

"It's not really his scene," he said for Frank's benefit.

"Bring him." It wasn't a request.

Pete clenched his jaw. If Frank didn't want to take the hint, fine. He wasn't his brother's keeper. He pushed past Frank and got into the front passenger seat of the car. Frank followed, squeezing into the back between the newest additions to the crew.

They cruised Northwest Industrial in silence. The tone of the evening hinged on Pete's mood, and the tension between him and Frank dampened the buzz.

"What's the matter," Pete said over the seat. "Lou busy tonight?"

Frank didn't respond.

"I hope it's worth it. Sacrificing yourself for a kid that isn't even yours."

Frank seemed confused by the word *sacrifice*.

"He has a name."

"Yeah, I know. He's *my* son."

"And you want nothing to do with him. Besides, this isn't about them. I'm here for you."

Pete glanced over at Kez then back at his friend.

"That's not how this works."

Pete began distributing rat tabs. He put one in his mouth. Stuck out his tongue. A cartoon rat with a human face grinned at Frank.

"Here's to old friends and new experiences."

Frank put the tab on his tongue with a shaky hand. Even though he'd done more than his share of recreational drugs, he didn't know what to expect from this trip, and that worried him.

The transition itself was a smooth one. One moment they were driving around the derelict streets of Northwest Industrial, the next they had slipped the bounds of time and place to find themselves within the house. All of them except Pete.

—new guests enter these hallowed halls/i focus the eye as my acolytes lead them deeper into the confines of the house—

—the one called frank runs his hand along the wall, the sacred inscriptions carved therein/I shudder at the touch/the souls within scream—

—the acolytes lead our guests towards the heart of the house/my heart/a circular room lacking both windows and doors/they do not enter/they are suddenly within when previously they had been without—

—they join the throng of previous guests/withered/beaten/yet unable to stop their ministrations/begging for relief they shall never receive/not even when the rift is permanently opened and their world becomes ours—

—at first the one called frank merely watches/playing the voyeur/i watch him watch/i allow him access to the eye and he watches himself/shocked at his own lack of inhibition—

—the throng of bodies parts to reveal kez, naked except for a hooded cloak/ her swollen belly protrudes from within/navel stretched and distended, the linea negra bisecting her abdomen into two hemispheres—

—my shadow child—

—the one called frank reaches out/places a hand upon her stomach/a constellation of bruises swirling below the surface of her skin—

—the child can be yours, she tells him/she moves his hand to her breast/heavy with poison and says, as can I—

—frank trembles/an image appears/our guest standing next to a woman on a porch/an infant in his arms—

—bring him to me kez tells frank—

—no, he says—

—no, i repeat—

—a tremor runs through these walls/my walls—

—one for one, kez says, bring us your son—

—he's not my son, frank says—

—he is not your son, i repeat—

—the house rumbles/the acolytes moan but do no cease their ministrations/kez drops the cloak and pulls the one called frank to her breast—

—please, he whimpers, don't make me—

—DO NOT, i repeat—

—walls constrict and dust falls/the room darkens—

—it must be done, kez whispers into frank's ear/he is no longer our guest/just hers/

—i will not allow it, i say, the child is mine to give—

—the souls within the house scream as i collapse upon myself/like a dead star under the weight of its own gravity/the acolytes continue to writhe/ pressing their bodies into one another as the walls press into them/the ceiling caves in and frank pulls away from kez/barely avoids being crushed/kez screams—

—bring him to me, she says—

—NO, i bellow, THE CHILD IS MINE—

—then the eye blinks out/and all is dark—

Pete Gilman came to somewhere in the bowels of Northwest Industrial, hand pressed tight against his beating heart. Only it wasn't his hand. He lifted his head and came face-to-face with a pink murine nose, cautiously sniffing the dried vomit on his chest. His arms and legs surprised him by flailing of their own accord, sending the rodent scampering off in another direction. The soreness of his moving limbs rivaled the pounding in his head.

That must have been some party, he thought as he rolled into a sitting position. He tried to conjure up an image of the night's festivities, but drew a literal blank—an expanse of matte black nothingness where his memory should be.

He limped his way to familiar territory, then lucked out and caught a cab. He didn't have any money on him, but swore an oath that he'd let the driver escort him inside the house to retrieve payment while the meter ran.

He muted the screen in the backseat and closed his eyes. *This was it,* he thought. *No more partying.* He needed some sleep, some weed, and a burrito. And then some more sleep. The thought of calming down calmed him. He pulled out his phone and texted Frank. *Time to detox,* he wrote. *Burrito later?* He hit send and smiled. Frank would hold him to it. If he held Frank to holding him to it.

One long blink later and the cab pulled up in front of his house. The driver threw it in park and bounced a concerned look off the rearview mirror. Two police cruisers blocked the driveway.

Shit, Pete thought. He did not need another parole violation.

Or maybe this was a good thing. He'd get cleaned up and get his life back on track. A faint paternal echo sounded in the far corner of his mind. Maybe he'd even consider settling down and spending some time with his son. Yeah, that wouldn't be so bad.

Pete instructed the driver to wait in the car, but the man insisted on going inside. The sight of three uniformed police officers having coffee with Pete's mother greeted them as they entered the kitchen.

"Sorry," Pete said. "Didn't realize you had guests." All three cops stood to their feet.

"Where is he, Peter?"

He hadn't expected that. *Where have you been?*, maybe. But not *Where is he?*

"Where's who?"

Mrs. Gilman slammed her hand on the kitchen table, her voice rising in pitch.

"Where's *Toby*, Peter? What have you done with him?"

A light clicked on, illuminating the black canvas in his brain. Frank, on his knees, naked, in front of Kez's pregnant stomach, the house crumbling around them. Her whispering into his ear.

—it must be done—

"Frank. . ."

He went for his phone. The officers' hands went to their hips. His text to Frank hadn't gone through. The phone fell from his hand as two of the officers wrestled him to the ground. The cab driver took that as his cue to leave. The third officer chased after him.

"You're trying to blame this on Frank?" Tears ran down Mrs. Gilman's face. "He was found dead in an abandoned lot *three days ago.*"

Life is a collapsing building no one can escape, Pete thought, from underneath a pile of cops.

Pete sat in the back of the police cruiser, hands cuffed behind him. He ignored the metal digging into his skin. If Frank was dead, who had taken Toby? They never showed you this stuff in those drug commercials. The part where your body became a soul-devouring portal to another dimension.

He looked up as they stopped at a light. A '68 Cadillac idled across the intersection. What were the odds? He tried to remember the color of Kez's car, but he'd only seen it during the night, usually while high.

The light turned green and the officer behind the wheel gave it the full two seconds before stepping on the gas. By that point the Caddie had rolled clear across the intersection. Pete turned his head and watched it go by. A woman with hair black like leather sat behind the steering wheel. She kept her eyes on the road in front of her as she passed, so he didn't get a good look at her face. The person in the passenger seat leaned forward to look at Pete. Pete couldn't identify the person because they wore a rubber rat mask.

A moment later Pete found himself doubting what he'd seen. He looked down at his chest, the last place he'd seen an actual rat. There, stuck to a dried crust of vomit on the front of his shirt, was a perfectly good rat tab.

He looked up to see if the police had noticed. This was it. His ticket to figuring out what had happened to Toby and Frank. He tucked his chin into his neck and groped for the tab with his lips. He stuck out his tongue as far as it would go.

"Oh, for Christ's sake, that's disgusting."

Pete looked up, tongue extended, and met the eyes of the driver in the rearview mirror.

"We'll get you something to eat at the station," the cop said. "Just put your tongue away."

"Tha-wee, offither." Pete pulled his tongue back into his mouth. The tip tasted of sick. He looked back down at his chest but didn't see the rat tab. He worked up a gob of spit inside his mouth and swallowed.

Joshua Chaplinsky is the Managing Editor of LitReactor.com. He has also written for popular film site Screen Anarchy and for Chuck-Palahniuk.net, the official website of *Fight Club* author Chuck Palahniuk. He is the author of *Kanye West—Reanimator*.

His short fiction has been published by *Zetetic*, *Motherboard*, *Vol. 1 Brooklyn*, *Thuglit*, *Dark Moon Digest*, *Pantheon Magazine*, and on the *Great Jones Street* app. More info at joshuachaplinsky.com and @jaceycockrobin on Twitter.

STAR WARS EPISODE VIII: THE LAST JEDI
The Changing of the Guard

A Gehenna Post Review

(Originally published on the Gehenna Post)

Greetings from the Ether,

The immortal franchise of *Star Wars* has seen many highs and lows, between the original trilogy's achievements to the prequel trilogy's lackluster execution. One thing that has remained consistent with the series is the general consensus between audiences and critics. In *The Last Jedi*, a schism has occurred. Audiences are divided down the middle with *Episode VIII*, while critics have lauded it as the best chapter since *The Empire Strikes Back*.

So why such a divided response? The most common explanation references the nature of *The Last Jedi*, how it puts to rest previous formulas of the franchise. In *Episode VII: The Force Awakens*, the few negative responses for the film cited its formulaic structure which paralleled *Episode IV: A New Hope*. Now, the negative responses to *The Last Jedi* cite its differences to previous installments as the primary flaw. Couple that with the hype and fan theories, the success of *The Force Awakens*, and this brought expectations to an all-time high. *The Last Jedi* is a film that is self-aware of fan's expectations, and purposefully chooses to ignore them. The twists and turns are not only unexpected, but downright shocking. In some ways pleasantly shocking, in others disappointing.

This disappointment originates with self-created expectations, and this is perhaps why the negative responses are, for the most part, unwarranted. *The Last Jedi* presents to *Star Wars* fans a changing of the guard. The death of the old ways, of the formulas and plot structures that we are all used to in this franchise. The characters that we have come to love make decisions and act upon events in ways that we are not accustomed to. But why would one of the most progressive franchises of all time be hated for drastically changing the fantastical universe we have all come to love?

The best way to describe *The Last Jedi*, is that fans who don't want change and want things to stay the same, are frustrated with a film that presents changes and doesn't want things to stay the same. *Episode VIII* stands on its own and presents a unique atmosphere and plot to a franchise that has had trouble in these exact fields. The best way to approach the film is with zero expectations, zero fan theories, and an open-mindedness toward change.

As for the film itself, *The Last Jedi* is easily the most beautiful film we have seen in this saga. The direction is unique, camera angles during fight scenes epic in scale, and the colors and cinematography are the best we've seen in the *Star Wars* universe to date. The characters all take interesting directions in their journeys and we are introduced to sides of these beloved characters that we have yet to see. The action is stunning, even if the plot at times is dull. The strangest aspect of *Episode VIII* is that the scale of the plot is minuscule compared to the scope of the characters. We find ourselves in a much more character-centered story than before. While the events that take place are significant to the development of the universe, the actual happenings are small in comparison to what happens between the cast and characters.

The changing of the guard happens in several instances, where we see what some call the death of a franchise, and others call the beginning of a new direction. There are subplots that don't quite fit, a couple forced relationships, and some scenes that don't quite make sense. These moments don't take away from the big picture, however. As soon as we find ourselves distracted and out of focus from the primary story with these subplots, we are yanked back into the fray.

All of the cast are superb for the most part, a few of the actors not really given a chance to shine. Character development is the focus of the story, and it works beyond expectations, delivering a climax that only opens the gateway to a fresh new direction within the beloved franchise. Is *Episode VIII* as good as critics say? Probably not. Is it as bad as the audience scores read? Absolutely not. *The Last Jedi* stands above the *Force Awakens* and *Rogue One*, but fails to dethrone *The Empire Strikes Back* as the best in the saga.

Our recommendation? Clear your mind before seeing the movie. Ignore the hype and the fan theories. Embrace change. The changing of the guard has happened, and we are excited to see where the new generation will take us.

OUR RATING: 4/5 STARS

THE
FISHERMAN

A NOVEL

JOHN
LANGAN

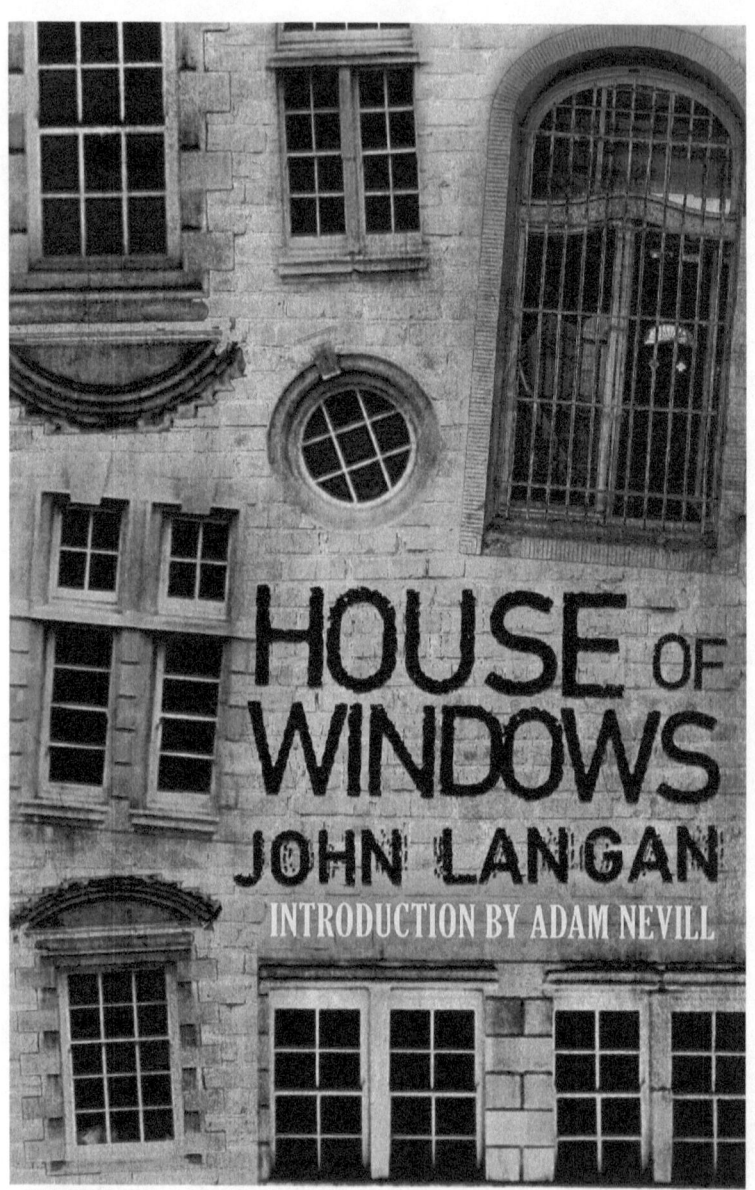

HOUSE OF WINDOWS

JOHN LANGAN

INTRODUCTION BY ADAM NEVILL

ORDER JOHN LANGAN'S *HOUSE OF WINDOWS* TODAY!

If you enjoyed **Hinnom Magazine**, make sure to leave a review on Amazon and follow us on social media!

Facebook: www.facebook.com/gehennaandhinnom-books
Twitter: www.twitter.com/GehennaBooks
Website: www.gehennaandhinnom.wordpress.com

Check out our other 2017 releases!

June 30th, 2017

Hinnom Magazine Issue 001

August 31st, 2017

Hinnom Magazine Issue 002

September 30th, 2017

Year's Best Body Horror 2017 Anthology

October 31st, 2017

Hinnom Magazine Issue 003

November 30th, 2017

Year's Best Transhuman SF 2017 Anthology

December 31st, 2017

Hinnom Magazine Issue 004

www.ingramcontent.com/pod-product-compliance
Lightning Source LLC
Chambersburg PA
CBHW030631130626
46552CB00002B/792